MY BROTHER'S FORBIDDEN FRIEND

PIPER RAYNE

About My Brother's Forbidden Friend

I've gone from crushing on my brother's best friend to wanting to crush him.

Cameron Baker and I have a few things in common. The first being that we were both born and raised in our small Alaskan town. Second, is that we hide our feelings and keep our hearts closed off from anyone who could break them.

But hiding my feelings is harder to do with Cam than most. When I was five years old, grieving the loss of my mother, he showed me how big his heart is, and I've never forgotten.

He comes from the richest family in town. Cam's bad boy gorgeous, flirts like he has a Doctorate in charm, and he's my brother's best friend. That last part is where it gets tricky and the sole reason we've never crossed the line.

Now, his parents have cut him off to force him to prove himself. I never thought he'd open a competing business to mine. So, I do what I do best, shove all my feelings aside and ready myself to crush him. Game on.

my brother's
FORBIDDEN FRIEND

The Greenes

Hank's Kids
Cade Greene (37)
Co-owner Truth or Dare Brewery
Fisher Greene (35)
Sheriff
Xavier Greene (33)
Pro Football Player
Adam Greene (31)
Forest Ranger
Chevelle Greene (30)
Water Boat Tourist

Marla's Kids
Jed Greene (37)
Co-owner of Truth or Dare Brewery
Nikki Greene (34)
Radio Host
Mandi Greene (32)
Owner of SunBay Inn
Posey Greene (28)
Owner of Fringe

Hank and Marla's Kid
Rylan Greene (17)

Chapter One

Chevelle

My first crush on a boy started when I was five years old, after I'd caused my mother's death.

I think a lot of girls have that one all-consuming crush. The one guy she never forgets and just can't seem to shake.

Unfortunately, mine is my brother Fisher's best friend, Cameron Baker. I never even wrote his name in my diary for fear of my crush being discovered. It doesn't help that he's five years older than me and isn't the settling down type. Which would be fine with me—I'm not looking for marriage either—but if I hooked up with Cam, my brothers would have something to say about it. To him and to me.

I was too young to get those butterflies in my stomach when my crush started, but it was the first time I didn't see him as another older brother who just wanted to boss me around.

After the "accident," my mom's wake was being held at our house. I can remember it all like it was yesterday.

I was sitting on my swing set in the dead of winter, wearing a purple dress that was too small for me. I'd worn it the year before when we visited some relative of my mom's who lived in the lower forty-eight. My hair was off-center in a knotted ponytail at the back of my head, after my grandma had fought my snarled hair for twenty minutes.

"There you are." Cam came out the back door of our house. He was dressed in a suit much like the ones my brothers wore, but his pants didn't sit inches above his ankles and his jacket didn't look as if the stitches were going to break.

While my mom usually passed down the suits from brother to brother, they didn't have a lot of reason to wear them in our small Alaskan town. We weren't poor, but when my dad had said he was going to take us all shopping to buy presentable clothes for the funeral, we fought him long enough that he retreated to his room, as he did a lot, and he never brought shopping up again.

"Is someone looking for me?" I asked.

I didn't want to go back in there. I felt like everyone was blaming me for the fact that my mom had fallen through the ice on the lake and died. They were right to blame me. It was my fault for wandering out there in the first place.

"Yeah." He smiled, the one where his left dimple indented. "I was."

He trudged across our yard with his big boots on and sat on the swing next to me, setting a plate of food on his lap. My stomach growled, and his smile deepened as if he was satisfied with himself.

Picking up a meatball on a toothpick, he held it out to me, steam rising off it from the cold air. "Want one?"

I shook my head.

"Come on. I can't eat all this."

I looked at his plate. Cam was known to eat all of our food, and he always asked for seconds when he came over for dinner. But I was hungry, and I didn't want to go inside, so I accepted it.

After my first nibble, I mumbled, "Thanks."

He continued to offer me food, blabbering about how he didn't realize the egg rolls had so much cabbage in them and that he didn't like cabbage. Or how his mom told him he couldn't have any more sweets for the day, so he had to sneak the brownie that was on his plate.

"Are you cold? I can get your jacket."

I was a little cold, but I'd been numb since the day my mom had died and I didn't much mind the biting cold on my skin. I shook my head. "If I sneak into my bedroom, will you not tell anyone?"

"I'll do one better. I'll help you."

"I don't need help. Just say you don't know where I am if someone asks."

I got off the swing and walked to the side of the house, where my mom had installed a white ladder thing last year. In the summer, it would be covered in green ivy. I remember the day before she died, she made a joke to my dad that they'd have to take it down when I became a teenager. I tried to commit everything I could from those last days to memory.

I started to climb the ladder but looked down at Cam. "Don't look up my dress."

He chuckled as if that was the most absurd thing and held his hands up, stepping back. Seeing my seriousness, he sobered. "I won't."

I eyed him once more, then climbed the ladder. When I was straddling my windowsill, I looked down at him. "Thanks for the food."

I climbed the rest of the way in and shut my window before he could say anything else.

The next few years weren't great for me. I was a little obsessed with always wanting to be with my dad and ended up seeing a therapist. Everyone walked on eggshells around me, but Cam was always there to lighten the mood with a joke. I gravitated to him when he came over, even if it meant just sitting in the same room and playing Barbies while the guys played video games. He'd make me forget that I felt like the reason the heart of our family was missing.

Years later, when those butterflies came, I didn't really know what to do. Because at the same time as I started to thrive off his attention for a different reason, Cam started to discover girls, and one never seemed to be enough.

Now, as I walk down the dock toward my boat—which I only have one more year of payments on before she's all mine—I mentally prepare myself for another fishing excursion with a bachelor party. At first I enjoyed them. Bachelor parties were always entertaining, and I could charge top dollar for the experience. Plus, I grew up with four brothers, so I was used to being the only girl. But lately, I've grown annoyed with the immature behavior of these men who need to celebrate the groom's freedom as if the old ball and chain is going to lock him in a closet for the rest of his life.

Someone whistles at me from a nearby boat. I look to find a fishing boat I'm familiar with.

"Careful there, Vic. I might have to tell Polly you aren't behaving yourself," I joke, knowing it wasn't him. He's old enough to be my grandpa.

Vic holds up his hands and points at the guy next to him. Must be a greenhorn because he doesn't look familiar. The way they find these guys and fly them in to see if they can handle the wicked weather out on the seas surprises me.

"Get to work," a voice yells from behind me.

A voice I recognize. That's why I deliberately pretend I don't hear him.

Cam follows me for a few steps. "So, you're ignoring me?"

I purposely increase my speed which isn't easy since I'm

carrying a case of beer in my hands. "We've been over this. I can fight my own battles out here."

"I just told them to get to work. I'm technically their boss."

I shake my head. "You aren't their captain."

"Jesus, Chevelle." He grabs my wrist and spins me around.

"Careful there, Baker. She's got a tough right hook," someone shouts from the boat. I can't be sure who it was.

Cam doesn't grant them an ounce of his attention, keeping his gaze on me.

I raise my eyebrows, and he huffs, as if I should know why he's tracking me down on the dock.

"Yeesss?" I draw out.

"I was just checking the log. Another boat full of guys?"

I roll my eyes. "No one ever told me we couldn't have orgies on the boat. Then again, is it an orgy if it's just me? I guess that's probably a gang bang, right?"

I watch his muscled chest expand with a deep inhale. You'd think I was being serious with the way he's reacting. "We've been over this. It's not safe."

I glance at my boat and back at him. "Did we become business partners, and I forgot? I'm not sure why you think you have a say in how I run my business."

"It's my job to protect you. I'm your brother's best friend."

I groan. "Have you not noticed that I'm a grown woman now, Cam?"

His gaze falls to my chest for a moment, and I bite my lip to keep from smiling.

This is the game Cam and I are currently playing. In truth, I have no idea if Cam is interested in me for anything other than my body. He's not been one to settle down, even though all of the guys he used to party with—most of whom are my brothers—are all coupled up now. But we enjoy pissing each other off. I do it because, well, I'm pissed that he's always telling me what to do and what to wear and who I should date. Then again, maybe I'm pissed because I want him to fall on bended knee and tell me he's always been in love with me. That the reason he pays me so much attention isn't because he considers it his duty because of my brother, but because he cares about me.

"Yes, Chevelle, I'm not the only one who notices that your tits are out half the time."

I narrow my eyes. "Bye, Cam." I turn my back on him and walk down the dock to my boat.

The guys today asked for a sunset fishing excursion, which means they aren't really the fishermen they're pretending to be. We'll arrive back in town just as the bars are getting packed, and they'll migrate there and drink until closing time.

My boat isn't painted pink or purple or what some would consider a girly color. Although if it wouldn't have affected my business, I might've painted it that. It's yellow, blue, and burgundy, but mostly white.

I climb on board and head into the galley, setting the case of beer on the ground. I have the first beer in my hand to put on ice when Cam climbs on right after me.

"I'm sorry, you need to ask permission to board my boat." I put my hand on his chest. His rock-hard chest.

"I'm serious about these guys. One of these days, it's gonna end in disaster." He crosses his arms.

While most of the guys out here are dressed as actual fishermen—orange overalls, water boots, and other items to try to keep them dry—Cam is in khakis and a polo because his dad owns the marina and he's training Cam to take over.

One day Cam will be the man who decides what I pay to dock my boat here. Perish the thought.

"It's my business. I cannot keep going over this with you, Cam." I stack the beer in the cooler, then head to the fridge to start the snack boards. All of my excursions come with food and beverages if they choose, and the bachelor parties always choose them.

"I'll go with you." He sits down.

I laugh somewhat manically, because I'd be seeing pigs fly rather than seagulls if I ever allowed that to happen.

"That's a hard pass." I tug at his arm, but he's too big for me to move.

"See how strong I am?" He arches an eyebrow.

"You fishing for compliments now?" I put the meat and cheese tray, along with the fresh sushi, back in the fridge before making sure the rest of the boat is clean and the poles are ready.

"I was proving my point." He comes up behind me.

I ignore the way a tingle races down my spine to my ass, as if I can feel the direction of his gaze.

Static comes over the outdoor speakers of the marina. "Cameron Baker, report to your office. Now."

We both look up at the windows in the building, and there stands his dad with both hands on his hips, staring down at us.

"What the hell does he want?" Cam mutters.

"Oh, Cam's in trouble. What happened? Did you take too much money out of the petty cash, or did you request a raise?" the fishermen shout various things from the decks of their boats, all of them laughing.

"This isn't over, Chevelle."

Cam stomps off my boat and back onto the pier, trudging toward the boathouse that's more of an actual office building. His dad's office is on the top floor, and Cam's is on the second floor, right smack in the middle.

"Have a great night, Cam." I wave with a smile just as the bachelor party walks toward me, reading the directions I gave them at top volume. Most already have beers in their hands.

Cam scowls at each of them as they pass.

"Welcome to Reelaxing Fishing Tours," I call.

"I told you I didn't want a stripper," the man who I presume is the groom says, needing my assistance to come on board.

"I didn't. She's the captain." The face of the man who booked me blotches red. "Sorry, they're already shit-faced, for the most part. I'm the designated sober ass for the day."

"Man, I was hoping she was a stripper," one of the other guys says.

I pretend to smile. Cam has a point, but I can take care of myself. I always have.

After my introductory speech and safety lecture, I start the engine and look toward the marina offices, where Cam is staring down at me. Maybe I'm so argumentative with him because it gives me his attention. I've always been a sucker for Cam's attention.

Chapter Two

Cam

I watch Chevelle's boat move farther out of the marina toward the gulf. She's knowledgeable and she knows her shit. I know she does. And I'm positive she's smart enough to have a gun somewhere on that boat, if not for protection from her charter guests, then from wildlife should anything happen if they pull up to one of the islands. Kodiak Island is no joke.

"Cameron!" My dad's booming voice from behind me doesn't startle the way it once did. I don't even turn my attention away from the window to greet him. "You keep chasing that Greene girl around."

That comment has me slowly turning around. "Chevelle. You know her name, Dad."

My dad disregards what I say. Not because he means disrespect to the Greene family. He should be thankful they gave me a realistic expectation of what a family is. Otherwise, I'd think it was normal to be left alone for the holidays while your parents go on vacation. Or even worse, maybe they drag you along by yourself since you have no siblings. Other than one time when I was fourteen and they let me bring Fisher to our house in Hawaii, anytime I was forced to go away with them, I was flying solo.

There were a lot of lonely times in my family. Mostly when all three of us were in the same room.

My dad sits on the sofa in my office and props one leg on top of his other knee. "It's time to embark on our next business venture, and I'd like you to head it up."

I rest my ass on the edge of the desk, crossing my ankles with my hands on either side of my hips. My gaze keeps diverting outside, even though Chevelle and her boat full of piss-drunk guys won't be back for about two hours and thirty-seven minutes.

Hey, it's my job to know when every boat leaves and comes back. It's standard practice for boats like hers to log their trips so that if they run into trouble and don't return, someone knows where to look.

"What next business venture?" I ask.

"Rowdy didn't make rent."

That causes me to focus on my dad. "What?"

"You know Rowdy, who tried to decrease prices with the hopes his business would pick up? He said it's his last month. He's done."

Unlike my dad, who only thinks of an open marina spot as a chance to jack the rent on the next person, I hate seeing people go out of business. Especially a guy like Rowdy, who's been here since before I was born.

"I think we should cut him a deal." I scan the marina once again.

My dad shakes his head. "You gotta harden that soft spot, son. There's no place in business for it."

"Well, there's something to be said for old-timers. I know Rowdy has helped Chevelle over the years. He mentors the young people who come in and will eventually take over."

A long, exhausted sigh leaves my dad's lips. "Let's put

Rowdy aside for right now. It's time we start our own touring business, and I want you to run it."

"Why, when we have two charter companies at the marina already?"

"Because Rowdy probably won't be here much longer and because it's a thriving business and I'm not one to ignore an already successful business model. Plus, you need to learn what it's like to start a new business before I just hand you mine." He raises his graying eyebrows.

My dad's been holding the reins of the company for years even though my mom wants him to take more time off.

"What do you have in mind?" I ask.

"Let's face it, Sunrise Bay isn't the same Podunk fishing town it once was."

"Like when you came and snatched the entire marina up for yourself?" I shouldn't be snide with my dad. It never ends well. But I'm feeling protective over Chevelle again, and the last thing I'd ever be comfortable doing is putting her out of business.

"I haven't heard you complaining when you use the money I've made to live the life you do." Both those gray eyebrows shoot up and I glance away. "That's what I thought. Anyway, it would be different than Chevelle's. We wouldn't be focusing on horny Joe Blows looking for a party. We'd be catering to a more sophisticated clientele. Sure, there'd be fishing, but that would come secondary to the cocktails and caviar on board."

I don't ask for further clarification because I'm not even entertaining the idea anyway.

"I figure since we're in the middle of tourist season right now, we can have a soft opening before the season's over."

"And what about my responsibilities here?" I look around my office.

"I'll take them over—for now."

I squeeze the bridge of my nose. "And if I refuse?"

He stands from the sofa and follows my line of vision out toward the bay. "Then you'll be cut off."

He's threatened for years to cut me off financially and it's never gonna happen. There's no way he'd leave his legacy to anyone but his only son. No fucking way.

"How about I think about it? Give me two weeks or so to finish off the sablefish season. Then we can talk."

He places his hand on the doorknob to my office. "I'll order the boat."

I open my mouth, but he's already on the other side of the door, walking down the hall and whistling like one of the seven dwarfs. God, the guy aggravates me to no end.

The pressure of having to prove myself to him is never ending. I sit behind my desk and pull up Rowdy's account. Screw my dad. I take my wallet out of my back pocket and grab my bank card. A few seconds later, Rowdy's account is paid in full.

I know it's not a long-term solution and it's only a Band-Aid on a widening hole, but it buys me some time to think of a plan.

MY OFFICE PHONE RINGS, but I don't have to answer to know who it is. It's the same guy who's called my cell phone five times, and I would answer, but it's now been two hours and forty-eight minutes since Chevelle left with those guys.

I can't hold Fisher off forever though, so I pick up. "Cameron Baker."

"What the fuck? I barely get time away from my house these days and you're late."

I hear the patrons of Truth or Dare Brewery, Fisher's brothers' bar in the background.

"I got caught up at work, but I'm coming."

"I'm finishing this beer and then I'm out, so hurry." He hangs up without telling me if he's one sip from being done or holding a brand-new beer.

The universe must be on my side because I spot Chevelle pulling into the harbor.

I try not to let my presence be seen through the window, so I turn off my office light and watch the boat pull into the dock.

One of the dipshits is throwing up over the edge of the boat, his dumbass friends laughing at him. Then I catch a guy standing with Chevelle in the wheelhouse while she brings in the boat. He's standing way too close for my comfort, so I grab my keys and my light jacket, heading down there.

By the time I make it down the elevator and out the doors, two of his friends have the one guy between them as they escort him down the pier, all of their drunken friends following.

All except the guy who was with Chevelle a minute ago. He's on the deck, talking to her, so I approach them.

"I'm really sorry. Let me pay you for cleaning costs." He pulls out a wad of cash, licks his thumb, and pulls out three hundred dollars.

"It's okay, honestly. Your deposit will cover the cost. Just don't expect to see it refunded on your credit card."

He chuckles and holds out the bills. "Please. I feel horrible."

She smiles and accepts the money, which means it must've been one horrible charter for her because that's not like Chevelle at all.

"I'm pretty sure they're going to crash right out. Maybe the two of us could—"

Over my dead body.

"You ready?" I interrupt.

Both of them turn toward me as though they didn't hear me approaching.

"Oh," the guy says.

"Cameron Baker." I hold my hand out between them.

"Cam," Chevelle says with that bite in her tone that makes me want to swing her over my shoulder.

"Hey, unfortunately my friends got too drunk and left her boat like this." He gestures to the side, and I see vomit, spilled beer, and cheese and crackers everywhere.

"It's nothing, honestly. Bachelor parties are always a little crazy." She smiles at no-name guy since he didn't have the courtesy to give me his name after I introduced myself.

"Craig!" the guys from the party shout.

He glances at them and back at us. "Thanks a lot. We really appreciate it, and I'll be sure to give you five stars on Yelp." He winks and earns another killer smile from Chevelle.

I suck in a deep breath, my nostrils flaring when I exhale.

"Thank you," she says.

"You better get going because there's a heavy fine if someone throws up on the pier," I say.

Chevelle narrows her eyes at me. I shrug.

"Really? I would think it's pretty common," the idiot says.

"Most people around here have sea legs." My voice is smug, but I don't care.

"You better go. The whole group looks like they're waiting for you," Chevelle says.

"Okay." He rocks back on his heels and looks at Chevelle, at me, and back at Chevelle. "Thanks again. Next time I'll make sure there's no one who can't handle their alcohol."

"That would be nice. Bye."

"Bye, Craig," I say pointedly.

He glances at me but walks down the pier to join his idiot friends.

"Why are you acting like you're my boyfriend or something?"

I grab the hose attached to the pier, turn on the water, and step into her boat. "I'm looking out for you. Your boat is in later than expected and that guy could've been some creepo."

She shakes her head but doesn't refuse my help cleaning. We work together and get it done in a half hour.

"I'll come back tomorrow and finish it up. I'm exhausted," she says.

I put the hose back and carry the garbage bags while we walk down the pier.

"Thanks, Cam," she says on our way out.

"You're welcome."

We're actually civil with each other until another figure approaches us at the marina exit.

"Chevelle." The guy stands in the shadows. For a moment, I think it's that douche Craig again, but when he gets closer, I see that this guy isn't in docker shorts and a polo. He's in jeans that hang off his hips and a threadbare T-shirt.

"Derek," she says with a lift in her voice that I don't care for. She rushes to him and hugs him. His eyes remain on me over her shoulder the entire time.

"Who's your friend?" he asks her.

"I could ask the same thing." I lift my chin a bit while I stare him down.

She steps back. "Sorry, this is Cam, my brother Fisher's best friend. Cam, this is Derek, my..."

He sticks out his hand. "Boyfriend."

What the hell? I've seen this guy around recently. He just went from Vinny's boat to Porter's. Definitely a douchebag if Vinny already got rid of him.

I shake his limp hand. "I didn't know Chevelle had a boyfriend."

"Well, she does." He widens his stance and crosses his arms as though he's claiming his territory.

Well, this is my territory, and Chevelle's been mine for a helluva lot longer than she's been his. Besides, I could easily kick the shit outa this little pissant.

"I haven't told a lot of people yet. Keep my secret?" She bats her eyelashes at me.

"You know I can't keep it from your brother and..." I lift my wrist. "I'm really late in meeting him."

"Let's go," Derek says to her. "The movie."

"Yeah, right. Thanks again for your help, Cam."

I nod, narrowing my eyes at Derek. Chevelle laughs as if my big-brother overprotectiveness is cute to her. She usually hates it. It's how I get a rise out of her most times. I like annoying her as if we're eight on the playground. Any reaction from Chevelle will do. At least it means she feels *something* for me.

The two of them walk off right as my phone buzzes in my pocket.

"I'm coming," I answer and hang up.

A short time later, I walk into Truth or Dare Brewery, ignoring everyone's hellos and heading right to Fisher, who's sitting with Jed, Chevelle's stepbrother.

"Did you two know Chevelle has a boyfriend? Some fisherman from the dock?" I say.

They stare at me for a beat, then look at one another.

"We all know Chevelle, it won't last," Fisher says.

Then they go back to their drinks. I sit quietly and stew, when what I really want to do is follow Chevelle and Derek on their date so I can make sure he's worthy of her.

Chapter Three

"Cocktease."

-Derek

Chevelle

My sister Mandi is getting married in two days. Since she and her fiancé, Noah, have been living in our shared house, I've yet to really invite Derek over because although he's really easy on the eyes, his personality is hard to warm up to. He has a chip on his shoulder that I'd love to help him shed. But other than that, he's been great.

I invited him over tonight since I'm the only one here.

The doorbell rings and I wait a few seconds before answering the door. A girl never wants to seem too eager for her date to arrive.

Derek has boxes of microwave popcorn, Junior Mints, and Skittles in his hands. "The musts of a movie night."

"I baked some cookies too. And I have popcorn. Great minds think alike."

He smiles and wraps an arm around my waist forcefully, pulling me into him. My hand lands on his chest and he smashes his lips to mine, sticking his tongue in my mouth without any finesse, just brute force. So he needs a little help in the kissing department. Good thing for him, I'm an expert teacher.

I slide out of his grip and take the items from him, heading into the kitchen.

"You bake?" he asks.

"Yeah. Ever since I was young." My brothers would always ask me to bake for them. They had to help me at first, but then I took over for most of the holidays.

He leans his ass against the counter and crosses his arms, watching me move the cookies from the cookie sheet to the cooling rack. "I never pegged you as a baker."

I chuckle. "How did you peg me?"

His gaze travels down my body. "Not as a baker. If I wasn't watching this with my own eyes, I would've assumed you bribed someone else to bake them just to impress me."

My forehead scrunches. "That's a little insulting." I put down the spatula and stare at him.

He pushes off the counter and grabs me again, pulling me into him. "It's only because you're so sexy. I always think of girls who bake as the ones who can't get a date on Saturday night." He kisses my neck. "But you're too fucking hot to bake."

I feel my cheeks heat. "Thank you."

I don't move out of his arms, allowing his lips to skate across my skin. When his mouth reaches my ear, he whispers some raunchy words about what he wants to do to me tonight. We haven't slept together yet and I'm not sure I'm ready. I like him, but there are some red flags, so I'm using tonight to feel him out since he's a fisherman and could be gone tomorrow for a week or two.

"Let's move this to the couch," he says and grabs my ass, pulling me up to him, so I wrap my legs around his waist.

He drops me on the couch, but I sit up, not ready for him to lie down on me just yet. His hand slides along my cheek, his fingers weaving through the hair at the side of my face, bringing my face to his. Our lips meet and again, he's not patient enough to wait for me to invite his tongue into my mouth. We've only been seeing each other for a few weeks now and I feel like if I criticize him, it won't go over well, and it's not as if I don't enjoy the tongue action. I just would've preferred a slower pace.

His free hand grabs my breast over my shirt.

"Hold on," I say, wiggling out of his hands.

"What is it?" He doesn't let go. Instead he leans in, his lips exploring my neck and venturing down to my chest.

"I just... we have the movie to watch, and this is all moving pretty fast."

"Come on, you're kidding me, right?"

The front door opens, and the lights flicker on. "Oh, I'm so sorry," Mandi says.

I scramble out of his hold and off the couch. "Hey, Mandi. Um... this is Derek."

Derek glances over his shoulder and gives a halfhearted wave to Mandi.

"Hi, Derek." Mandi looks at me. "So, Noah is on his way home and we're going to Glacier Point for the night. Someone gave us a gift certificate, but we have to use it tonight."

I roll my eyes. "You know who it's from, right?"

She nods. "The grandmas. I figure Dori's grandson-in-law owns the resort, so they probably swindled some deal or badgered him until he finally gave in. You know what they're like."

All of my siblings are living their happily ever afters. And although I wouldn't mind having someone to do fun things with and maybe be a regular sex friend, marriage and all that stuff isn't a priority for me. But there are still those moments when I wouldn't mind having someone who loves me as much as my siblings' partners love them. "I hope one day I'm in the position to get all these luxury things."

Mandi raises an eyebrow. "Luxury things? Chevelle, need I remind you of your bridesmaid's dress?"

"Babe, I thought we were watching a movie," Derek says from the couch.

"In a minute." I hold up a finger.

He blows out an annoyed breath. Mandi glances at him and I see the question in her eyes. Why am I with him? He's not exactly being nice tonight. But this is a small town and there isn't a plethora of options for me either.

"You know they're doing this because they think it will seal the deal," I say.

Mandi's forehead wrinkles. "Seal the deal?"

"I know, right? If only they were in the room next door to you guys every night, they'd know how real your relationship is." The noises that come out of that room every night definitely make me want a permanent fuck buddy. If he could be as tall as Noah, that would make it better.

Mandi drops her bag. "You mean they don't think Noah and I are really together?" Her face flushes like it does when she's worried.

I shrug. "Just Dori and Ethel. They kept grilling me at dinner the other night, but I didn't think you'd want me telling Grandma that your screaming could wake a family of hibernating bears."

Her face grows redder, which I didn't think was possible. "Thank you for that."

The door opens and Noah comes in and spots Derek on the couch. "Who are you?"

Hearing the deep voice, Derek shifts to look behind him. "Who are you?"

Noah stares at Derek as if he's sizing him up. God, this is so uncomfortable.

"That's Derek." Mandi motions between him and me, and Noah nods at him.

"So, let me see this gift certificate," Noah says. Mandi pulls it from her bag, and he inspects it. "You can thank whoever this is from for your good night's sleep tonight." He winks at me.

The three of us laugh.

"Chevelle—movie?" Derek says in a stern voice.

Noah glances at Mandi.

"I said in a minute," I snipe.

Noah leaves Mandi's side and sits on the chair adjacent to the couch. "So, you're seeing Chevelle, huh?"

Derek barely glances in his direction. "Yeah."

"Are you from Sunrise Bay?"

"No, I'm just passing through."

Noah's eyes narrow. "I'm sorry?"

"I'm working on one of the fishing boats."

Noah nods, probably wondering what I see in Derek. I'm starting to have the same thought.

"Cool. Well, I guess I'll see you at the wedding." Noah gets up off the chair.

"Oh, you're the poor son of a bitch getting hitched, huh?" Derek laughs.

Mandi hits me with a death glare. Hey, marriage isn't for everyone.

Derek laughs some more. "Totally joking. Congrats, man, that's awesome."

Noah looks at Mandi. "Let's go, Mandi."

They go upstairs and I head into the kitchen for the cookies and popcorn. Derek follows me.

"I'm only hungry for one thing," Derek says, putting his fingers in the waistband of my shorts and pulling me toward him.

"They're still here," I whisper. I stand between his legs and his hands venture under my shorts and onto my ass cheeks.

"Get them out so I can get inside you," he whispers, kissing my navel that's showing with the crop top I'm wearing.

I guess now is as good of a time as any to tell him I won't be sleeping with him tonight. I open my mouth to speak, but Mandi and Noah come downstairs. Mandi eyes me and Noah acts as though we're not even here. He's got both their bags.

"I'll be in the car. Have a good night, you two." Noah stops at the door after it's open. "Just so you're aware, Chevelle's dad lives in the house on the hill across the street. And her brother is the sheriff."

"Noah..." I shake my head.

"Hey, no one else is here to be the protective brother for you. I'm about to be your brother-in-law, so it counts."

"Technically, stepbrother-in-law."

Mandi walks over to him, stuffing the gift certificate in her purse. "You know we don't act like step anything. I'd be more fearful of my mom than Hank though." She widens her eyes at Derek.

He says nothing and I kind of wish they were staying.

"Bye." I give them a small wave.

They both stare at us for a beat, then open the door and walk through it, shutting it behind them. I hear Noah's truck start up, then the engine noise dims as they pull out of the driveway.

My heart rate picks up.

Derek grabs my hand and tugs me onto his lap on the couch. "Finally alone. Where's your bedroom?"

"Um..." I place my hand on his chest. "I don't think I'm ready for that. Can we just watch the movie tonight?"

"You're not ready?" He laughs. "You're kidding, right?" He eyes my shirt and shorts.

"What? We barely know one another and I'm not ready to sleep with you."

He scowls. "Then why do you dress like that?"

I refrain from grabbing a blanket off the back of the couch and covering myself. "Because I like these clothes. Because they're in style. Because I think I look good in them."

He points at me. "Exactly, you look sexy as hell in them. You're showing off your body like you wanna get fucked."

I slide to the other side of the couch. "Well, I don't want to get fucked, and definitely not by you."

He huffs and his gaze diverts away from mine before he looks back at me, eyes full of anger. "You're a cocktease."

"Why would I be a tease? Did I just give you a hand job and right before you came say, 'Oh no, I don't do that'? No. I've given you no reason to think I wanted to sleep with you." I cross my arms. All the looks Mandi was giving me seem justified now. Once again, I chose to see the good in a shitty person.

"You dress with more skin showing than fabric. You invited me to your house for a movie. You've been all over me all night."

"Bullshit!" My voice grows louder. "You've been the one pawing at me all night. And I invited you over to watch a movie, not to sleep together." I stand and head to the front door, opening it wide. "You can go."

He stays where he sits on the couch. "I'm not going anywhere."

The first fissure of fear cracks my veneer. "You are." I try to keep my voice even and continue to stand with the door open.

He waits me out in silence, and I pretend to inspect my nails instead of wondering if I should call one of my brothers to help me. God, how embarrassing would that be? Poor little Chevelle can't take care of herself.

After a few minutes, he finally bolts up from the couch, hands in fists at his sides. "Fine. Your loss."

I raise my eyebrows. "Oh, I'm sure I'll be crying tonight."

He grabs his candy and microwave popcorn, walking past me. "Cocktease."

After he's gone, I slam the door and flick the lock, turning off the lights. I walk into the kitchen, grab the plate of cookies, and retreat to my room. Something has me picking up my family photo album and flipping through the pages, wishing for the millionth time that my mom was still here to give me advice.

I stare at the bridesmaid's dress hanging on my closet door. I'm the last one standing and I'm not sure if I like that or not. It used to not bother me at all, but now... I don't know. Then again, step one would be meeting a guy who's worth my forever. Sure, there's Cam, but he's not marriage material.

Chapter Four

Chevelle

'm getting ready for Mandi and Noah's wedding, take two, collecting my dress, my makeup bag, and everything I need to get ready when the doorbell rings.

Their original wedding didn't happen because Mandi called it off, but they've since worked out all their shit and are more excited than ever to be husband and wife.

I jog down the steps and open the front door, expecting it to be Nikki because she probably thinks I'm going to be late and feels like she needs to pick me up to keep me on schedule. But standing on the other side of the door is a man in a suit and holding a bouquet of flowers in front of his face. I can tell that it's Derek.

I haven't seen or talked to him in a few weeks.

When I don't say anything, he lowers the flowers away from his face and smiles brightly. I open my mouth to tell him to go away, but he holds up a hand. "Give me a chance to apologize?"

I close my mouth and wait for his words, but they aren't going to make much of a difference to me. I made the right call when I broke things off with him.

"I'm sorry I acted like an asshole. There's no excuse for me saying those things or acting like that to you. I've been stressed with the job on the boat. The guys are all being dicks to me. Then you have this whole big life here with all these people who love you and I don't have anyone. My parents sure as shit don't care about me. They don't even know where I am. I guess I was anxious for things to work out with you because I want someone on my side."

"You said I was a cocktease. How does feeling lonely account for you doing that?"

He looks at his feet, shaking his head. "I was mad because I felt judged by your sister and her fiancé, so I lashed out and said mean things to make you hurt the way I was. But I promise it'll never happen again. Just give me another chance. Please, Chevelle."

I look at him, really look at him, to see if he's sincere and I think maybe he is. My head says to tell him to leave, but my heart feels that tug as it always does when someone is asking to be forgiven. I mean, everyone deserves a second chance, right? No one is perfect. I know better than anyone what it's like to make a mistake.

My family doesn't know I broke off whatever we had because any time they inquired about him, I just said he was out at sea. If they knew we split so soon, they'd probably chalk it up to me picking a loser again.

"I'm so sorry. Please forgive me." He drops to his knees with a small smirk because he can probably feel me softening.

"Get up, Derek."

He stands and he's about to step into the house when I place my hand on his chest. "I have to go to the inn to get ready." I run my hand down my face, hoping I'm not going to regret this decision. "We can start off by you coming to the wedding with me."

"I was hoping you'd say that. I heard your sister's

wedding was moved to today. That's why I came prepared and dressed in a suit."

"I'm not saying everything is okay, but we'll go to the wedding and then we'll figure it out from there. Deal?"

He nods a bunch of times. "More than fair. And I'm going to treat you like a fucking queen. You'll never wanna let me go."

I give him a small smile. "I hope so. Can you drive me over to the inn?"

He steps out of my way and puts out his hand. "Your chariot awaits."

I grab my stuff and lock the front door then walk to his car and put everything in the back seat. He shuts my door and I put on my seat belt. I watch him walk in front of the car to his side and his smile is so wide. He looks so happy.

I can't imagine living with no family. No one on your side to care about you even when you screw up. I mean, my family still loves me even though it's my fault my mom is dead. What could Derek have done for them to disown him like that? But I don't want to broach that conversation today when we're trying to repair things between us.

After he pulls out of the driveway and starts down the road, he holds out his hand to me. I slide my palm into his and our fingers lock. His thumb runs along my forefinger.

"Thank you," he says with such an earnest expression that I no longer question my decision to give him a second chance. "I have to go to work after the ceremony, but I'll be back in a couple of days. Maybe we could go on a date?"

I smile at him. "I'd like that."

He tightens his hand around mine. "Good."

We arrive at the inn, and I give him a peck on the cheek before climbing out of his car and gathering my things.

"Can't wait to see you all dolled up," he says.

I don't bother to tell him that the senior citizens from the retirement home made our dresses and to temper his expectations. Rather, I say, "I'll be interested to hear what you think."

We smile at one another, a spring of hope running through my heart. Maybe I was too quick to judge him. He has some unresolved issues in his life. Who doesn't?

By the time I reach the room upstairs where everyone is getting ready, I'm the only one still in street clothes and not in their dress.

"Finally! Do you not have a clock?" Nikki says as soon as I walk into the room.

"I'm, like, five minutes late."

Marla, my stepmom, comes up and runs her hands down my hair. "Don't worry about it. You're here. I saw a young man drop you off."

Marla's a great stepmom. She's always been there for me, and even though I'm not her blood, she still senses when something is off with me.

"Yeah, it was Derek."

She smiles as if that spring of hope is running through her heart too. Everyone wants me to find my happily ever after, it seems.

"Every relationship starts somewhere." She kisses my cheek. "Now, go get dressed and ready. We're walking down in ten."

"Ten minutes?" I screech and start to strip off my clothes. "But I'm on time."

Marla helps me get in my dress, and I'm pushed into the makeup chair while Posey fiddles with my hair, putting it up with a bottle of hairspray and a box of bobby pins.

Before I know it, someone hands me a bouquet of flowers and I'm walking down the stairs of the inn toward the back patio area where the ceremony is taking place. Last I knew, it was a small gathering of just family and closest friends. Since our family probably takes up the entire space, it's a good thing Noah has such a small family.

I'm the first one down the aisle because although we don't refer to each other as stepsiblings very often, it is the truth that Posey and Nikki are Mandi's biological sisters. I'm completely fine with it though. Sometimes I wonder if my parents would've tried for more if my mom hadn't died. Maybe I would've had my own sister.

I smell cigarette smoke the minute I step onto the patio and catch Derek flicking the butt of his cigarette onto the pathway that runs along the shore of the bay below. I suppress an eye roll over the fact that he couldn't properly dispose of his cigarette butt or better yet, wait until after the ceremony to smoke. He scrambles to his seat.

Smacking on a smile, I hold my bouquet and walk down the aisle. After so many family weddings, I'm a pro at this.

Everyone watches me, and I smile at Derek, who doesn't smile back. Lord, he's so moody. What could have happened between him dropping me off and now that soured his mood so much? Maybe this won't work out between us. His moods swing like a pendulum and they're always unpredictable. I feel as though I never know what I'm going to get with him.

I look to the groom's side as a distraction, but obviously our side has had to take up space on his side. Cam is there. He's dressed in a dark suit and has my nephew Axel in his lap. Axel is fast asleep, sucking on his pacifier. Cam winks at me as though we're not usually butting heads, and my stomach does this weird whooshing thing, like waves reaching the shore.

God, he looks good with a baby. Too good. It could give a girl like me, who's had a crush on him forever, ideas.

I strip my eyes away before my ovaries explode and walk to the end of the aisle, turn left, and wait for the others. Posey and Nikki both make their way down, and soon Mandi is standing at the end of the aisle with my dad on her arm.

The turbulent relationship my stepsiblings have with their dad makes me even more grateful for the one parent I still have. I can't imagine my mom disappointing me like their dad does all the time. I'm the one who disappointed her when I went out onto that frozen lake. Those are feelings that even my therapist couldn't help me with.

My dad kisses Mandi's cheek and goes to sit next to Marla, leaving Mandi with Noah. They're a good-looking couple. They fit well together in personality and appearance.

We all listen to them say their vows and exchange rings. Posey tears up, and I hear some sniffles in the audience. I look to see which one of my sisters-in-law it is, but make the mistake of locking eyes with Cam. As Mandi slips the ring on Noah's finger and promises to love him until death do they part, I'm locked in his gaze. It's as if he knows how much those words affect me. How my parents said those vows probably thinking whoever died first would be gray and elderly. Maybe that would've been true if they'd stopped at four kids. But because of me, my mom died in her thirties, with five kids to raise.

Cam's soft expression somehow eases the pain piercing my heart. I've learned to live with these feelings that come over me at moments I wish they wouldn't. Usually I smile and pretend I'm not affected, only to lock myself in the bathroom for a few minutes, cry, and get over it. But I don't feel like crying right now. I feel like taking comfort in Cam's arms.

What the hell am I thinking?

The officiant announces them as husband and wife and they walk down the aisle, pulling me from my unwelcome thoughts.

We all file down the aisle and everyone heads toward the dining room. Derek meets me and we converse a little, but it feels forced. Any of the ease we had a short time ago is gone. He announces that it's time for him to leave and I decide to walk him to his car to say goodbye.

Mandi spots us on our way out. "Where are you going?"

"I'm just saying goodbye to Derek. He has to get to work," I say.

"Not sure who plans a wedding during the week," Derek grumbles.

My stomach falls to the floor. Yeah, we're definitely not going to make this relationship work.

"Stop it," I say. "How about a thank-you?"

Derek doesn't say anything. "Congratulations," he says to Mandi what feels like a lifetime later.

I see the scowl Mandi's trying to hide. She doesn't like him at all, but Mandi is always polite, so she puts on a smile. "Thanks. Sorry you can't stay." She's lying through her teeth.

"I'll be right back," I say and squeeze Mandi's hand.

Derek slides his hand in mine on the way to the car.

"Thank you for coming. You didn't have to," I say in an attempt to start this conversation on a positive note.

"I know I didn't."

At his car, he opens the door and stands in the doorway. "So I'll see you when I get back and we can make plans."

My lips press together. "Maybe we can talk first when you're back before we firm up plans."

He tilts his head and something about it feels slightly predatory. "Talk? What's there to talk about? I thought you forgave me?"

"Yeah, but..." Why couldn't I have just said goodbye and left it at that?

"But what?" His posture goes rigid.

"We'll talk when you get back. I need to get back in there." I kiss his cheek and step away.

He grabs my wrist. "Tell me whatever it is now." The words are laced with venom.

I sigh and look toward the inn full of people. Everyone is in the dining room, so there isn't anyone outside. "I'm not sure it's going to work between us. We're very different people."

"Why wouldn't it work?" He's still holding my wrist and his fingers press harder into my skin.

"Honestly? You're not very nice to my family. And like I said, we're different."

"Your family is always looking at me like they don't like me. Like they think they're better than me and they judge me because I'm a fisherman."

"They would never judge you for that. I'm practically a fisherwoman."

He scoffs. "Please... you strip down naked and take out bachelor parties. God knows what happens out there on the open water."

My mouth drops open. "Fuck you." I unwind my wrist from his grip and stomp off.

"What the hell did you just say to me?" He stalks after me, grabbing my upper arm and swinging me around.

"I said fuck you!" I shout. "We're over."

"Like hell we are." His hand comes up in a blur and I turn just as his fist connects with my face.

"You bastard!" I cover my eye as if that's going to make a difference. "Get the fuck out of here before I rip your balls off." I bend down, tears springing to my eyes.

"Shit. Shit. Shit." He bends down to hover over me. "I didn't mean to do that. I'm sorry. I really am. It's just that I really like you and I don't want you to break up with me."

I stand up straight. "Go to hell. Get outa here." I step back in case he comes after me again.

"Chevelle, I really didn't mean it. I'm sorry." It's like another personality has come over him—he's gone from rage to sorrow in a heartbeat.

"Go!" I point toward his car.

The door of the inn opens and a guy I think might work in the kitchen comes out, heading toward his car. He looks at the two of us, and Derek retreats to his car.

"Fine. Have it your way," he mumbles.

Once his tires are off the gravel of the parking lot and on the pavement of the road, I slide through the doors of the inn, heading to the bathroom and hoping my face isn't as bad as it feels. I feel equal parts shaken and numb. I've never had a guy be aggressive with me before. I don't quite know how to feel.

"Chevelle." Cam touches my arm as I pass by him.

I purposely keep my face down. "I have to go to the bathroom."

His forefinger and thumb touch my chin and he turns my face up, seeing what I assume is the start of a black eye because his eyes flash with concern first, then red-hot anger.

He touches around my eye gently and I wince. "Oh, he just wrote his fucking death certificate."

"I handled it, Cam, relax."

"Then I'll handle it again."

"Please don't," I say, but he's already walking out the doors of the inn as if he's the white knight who's going to save me.

Chapter Five

Cam

That asshole is a dead man. Worthless piece of shit. What kind of man hits a woman?

I climb into my car, my foot slamming on the brake as I hit the start button and put it in drive. My tires kick up gravel as I speed out of the parking lot of the inn. The entire drive to the marina, all I envision is my fist slamming into his jaw and the satisfying crunch I'll hear. I'll make sure he never touches her again.

I have no choice but to slow down as I roll through town, but once I'm out of the downtown area and closer to the marina, I kick it into high gear, racing into the parking lot before slamming on my brakes and stalking out of my car. I shed my suit jacket and toss it on the park bench that sits close to the marina. Porter's just came in from gold crab season by the Aleutian Islands and said he was going to do a cod run before he goes back out for more gold crab.

The guys are stacking the equipment for cod fishing when I approach Porter's boat. Derek's nowhere to be seen though.

"Hey, Porter."

The old man looks down off the deck of his boat.

"Permission to come aboard?"

He waves me up. "Little dressed up for a boat, no?"

"You have a deckhand. Derek something?"

He glances over his shoulder and blows out a breath. "What'd he do?"

I guess I'm that transparent.

The other deckhands slow their movements and look at us, eager to figure out why I'm looking for their new guy. They're good at sensing the ones who don't fit, so their radar is probably up on Derek anyway.

"I just need a word. He here?"

"In the barracks. Changing. This is his second time being late. One more strike and he's gone."

Porter has three daughters of his own. Once the news travels that Derek hit Chevelle, he'll be lucky if he's not chopped up and used as bait.

"You might want to call for a new deckhand then."

Porter's chin drops to his chest, and he shakes his head.

As luck would have it, Derek comes out of the door from the barracks and comes to an abrupt halt when he sees me. The cockiness he's worn as a badge isn't there anymore. He knows why I'm here.

"Listen. It was an accident. She's clumsy." He holds up his hands. "I don't know what she told you."

"Fucking hell," Porter mumbles.

"What kind of accident?" I approach him, hands fisted at my sides, pulse thrumming in my ears.

"Who is she?" a deckhand asks.

Neither of us answers, but they know me well and know who I'd protect within an inch of my life. Not that I wouldn't protect any woman, but I'd go above and beyond for Chevelle.

"The car door. She was saying goodbye and I was shutting the door. It was an accident."

I stalk toward him, and he steps back again. "That's not what she said."

In truth, she didn't say anything, but she didn't have to. I saw the embarrassment and shame all over her face—both of which she shouldn't be feeling. Just like at her mother's wake, she wouldn't make eye contact with anyone. She blamed herself for her mother's death and she probably blames herself for dating this douche.

"You know chicks like her. Always the victim even though they dress like that."

Adrenaline surges through my veins and it's all I can do to keep my voice even. "Dress like what?" I continue my approach.

His hands are still up in the air. "Like she wants it."

"And when she said no, you hit her?"

All the equipment the fishermen are holding falls to the deck of the boat, and they walk over behind me.

"I told you it was an accident." He's jittery, his eyes darting to the men behind me.

I appreciate the backup, but I'll handle this myself.

"It wasn't an accident. You fucking hit her, and now it's time to learn what it's like when someone a helluva lot bigger hits you." I cock my fist back and nail him right in the left eye.

Satisfaction filters into my bloodstream and I give him a wicked smile. He teeters a bit to the side, but I want him to come at me. I want any excuse I can get to beat the shit out of him.

"I said I was sorry, man." He touches his eye, blood squirting from where the skin broke open.

"Sorry isn't good enough. Didn't anyone ever tell you never to hit a woman?" I aim my fist for his face again, but he blocks me this time. So I hammer my left hand into his side. He hunches over.

"Fuck, man. If you want her, why didn't you just say so? Just so you know, she's a fucking cocktease though."

This idiot must have a death wish.

I rush him, tackling him around the waist and taking his legs out from under him. My fists hit anywhere I can make contact and he's trying to wrestle me to get me off him, throwing blind punches up.

"You touch her again and I will fucking murder you!" I continue my assault while he curls up in the fetal position, covering his face.

"Okay, Cam. Ease up. You made your point." Porter and another guy grab my arms, struggling to pull me off him.

When Derek stands, he wobbles, blood dripping from his face onto his shirt. God, he deserves so much worse.

"Don't call her. Don't go see her. You forget she even exists, do you understand me?" I shout, wiggling to get free so I can go after him again. The guys grip my arms tighter, keeping me in place.

"Get the fuck off the boat, Derek," Porter yells. "You're fired."

His head rocks back. "Why? Because of what this dipshit said?" He points at me.

"This dipshit owns the marina, you fucking asshole," I respond. "Go find somewhere else to work."

"He's right. They own the marina, but regardless, we don't let men who hit women on this boat. You got off easy, because if it was one of my daughters you hit, you'd be fish food." Porter points at the exit. "Now get off my fucking boat."

Derek shakes his head. "This whole town is a shithole. Good luck finding anyone else who would wanna live here and work for you." He walks over to the exit and gets off the boat.

"Boys, go get his stuff. I don't want any reason to have him coming back," Porter says.

A couple guys walk into the opening to the barracks. They return with a garbage bag and toss it onto the dock where Derek stands.

We all watch in silence as he leaves the marina. Once he's gone, I pull out my phone.

> Drop Chevelle off at home tonight. Don't let her leave by herself.

> Nikki: Okkkaaayyyy

I can tell she doesn't know why, but she doesn't ask any questions. Maybe she hasn't seen Chevelle's face yet. Regardless, I know for sure if Derek is waiting on Chevelle's doorstep tonight, Logan will deal with him appropriately.

I apologize to Porter for the disruption, then head to my parents' yacht to clean up.

A BANGING SOUND WAKES ME. "CAM!"

I open my eyes and blink a few times, trying to figure out where I am. My parents' yacht, right. Fisher stands on the other side of the glass door wearing his sheriff's uniform. I struggle to get up off the couch I crashed on. I might've won the fight with Derek, but he got in a few good shots too.

Fisher signals for me to open the sliding glass door.

"No shit," I mumble and flick the lock, opening the glass and heading back to the couch.

"What the fuck, man? How could you do this to me?" His hands rest on his hips and he looks at me with a scowl.

I scowl back. "Do what to you?"

He pulls his handcuffs from the back of his belt. "Cameron Baker, you're under arrest for the assault of Derek Latrell."

"You gotta be fucking kidding me." I push up off the couch. "Fish, man. You know I had to do it."

"Save it for the interrogation. I'm so pissed that you put me in the position of having to come seek you out on an arrest warrant." He takes my arms around to my back and handcuffs my wrists together.

"You know what he did to deserve it."

Fisher isn't listening. He gets on the radio to Johnson, telling him he found me and he's bringing me to the station.

He lets me slide on my shoes, but I have no shirt.

"You can at least let me get dressed," I say.

"I have to treat you like everyone else. I can't give you special treatment because you're my best friend." He leads me out the sliding doors and off the yacht, which is tricky as hell in handcuffs.

After he gets me onto the pier, we walk toward the parking lot. He holds my arm as if I'm going to try to escape.

"I get you're a tough-ass cop, but it's me, Fish. Is this a joke? You of all people should understand why I'd go after him."

"Okay, let's hear it then."

I open my mouth to respond, but my dad is stalking down the pier and stops in front of us. "What is this about now?" He blows out a breath, looking incredulous.

"Cam's being arrested for assault," Fisher says.

My dad runs his hand down the back of his neck and, if

possible, his cheeks get even redder. "Don't use your one call on me."

"You don't get it—"

He inches closer, lowering his voice since a crowd is forming. "What I don't get is why you can't put your nose down and just do your job. Learn the business and take it over. Now you're going to have a record. I'm done with it all, Cam. This is the last straw."

"But—"

"It's over. I'm taking back your apartment and your trust fund. Find your own place to live. I'm done babying you."

"Dad, you don't—"

My dad points his finger in my face. "Time to man up, son. You're on your own."

He walks by me, and Fisher sighs, shaking his head.

"Let's go." Fisher tugs on my arm and pulls me forward.

We walk up the ramp to the parking lot. He puts me in the back seat of the sheriff's truck while all the business owners in the downtown circle come out to figure out what all the commotion is about.

How am I the only one who knows Derek hit Chevelle? Didn't she tell her family after I left? Surely if Fisher knew the situation, he wouldn't be this pissed at me.

He buckles me in with a scathing look on his face, then he slams the door and rounds the truck to get in the driver's side. A few people ask him questions, but he doesn't answer, starting the ignition and pulling away toward the sheriff's station. I stare out the window, thankful he hasn't put on the sirens and caused more of a spectacle.

Ten minutes later, I'm in the interrogation room, but not with Fisher. He said that since his little sister's boyfriend was involved, he had to recuse himself, so he left me with Mato. At least my hands are free of the cuffs now.

"Can I please get a shirt?"

Mato rocks back in his chair, notepad in front of him. "Yeah, I'll get you one. But tell me why you attacked Derek."

"If Fisher would've let me explain, I would've told him. Derek hit Chevelle."

The two front legs of Mato's chair hit the floor and he stares at me for a beat. "Seriously?"

I throw my hands in the air. "Do I go around town hitting people? No."

"You can't deny the bar fights you get into sometimes."

"It's been almost a decade, Mato."

"Some reputations are hard to get rid of." He stands and straightens his belt. "I'll be back."

I watch him through the window as he goes over to where Fisher's standing in the hallway. I know the minute he tells him because Fisher glances in my direction. I shake my head in disappointment that he, of all people, didn't let me explain. Fish and his damn temper.

He stomps down the hallway, opens the door of the room I'm in, and slams it shut. "Seriously?"

I hold up my hand. "Swear to God."

"Well, fuck, this changes everything." And then he's gone again.

"Can I please call a lawyer?" I ask Mato, who's standing in the doorway.

"He doesn't need a fucking lawyer. Give me fifteen minutes and this will all be handled," Fisher shouts from his office, slamming the door.

"A lot of slamming doors today, huh?"

Mato shrugs. "Fisher's in today, so yeah. Tends to be quieter on his off days."

I can only imagine. I love my best friend, but he's got a temper. Mato forgets that I had a sidekick during a lot of those fights he mentioned, and it was none other than Sheriff Greene himself.

But I trust Fisher to get me out of this shitty situation. Then I remember my dad saying he was cutting me off. Probably already has my stuff from my apartment on the street by now. Fisher can't get me out of that situation.

Doesn't matter. Chevelle is worth it. No one will ever touch a hair on her head as long as I'm around.

Chevelle

News travels fast.

I'm getting out of the shower and deciding how I'm going to cover my black eye when Marla uses the key I gave her to enter the house with my dad.

"*Chevelle!*" my dad booms from downstairs.

I knew this would be a problem. I hid in the dim light of the wedding reception last night, and luckily, one of the makeup girls helped me cover the bruise enough for no one else to see it. I told her I took an elbow to the face by accident.

But I know that sound in my dad's voice. It's the same one he used when I broke curfew, or sneaked out, or he found boys in the basement. The "what the hell is going on" tone.

"I'm just out of the shower. Hold on."

I hurry up and dress in shorts and a T-shirt. I purposely didn't take any appointments for the boat today for fear that I'd be hungover. Turns out that's a good thing, because looking out the window, I see it's cloudy. Everyone would be looking at me as though I was crazy for wearing sunglasses.

I stare in the mirror one last time. There's no hiding this.

I walk down the stairs and into the kitchen, refilling my coffee mug. "Hey, guys," I say nonchalantly. "Want a coffee?"

"No." My dad's big footsteps pound on the floor until he's right in front of me. His fingers take me by the chin and tilt my face up. Not in the gentle way Cam did last night. "I'm gonna kill the bastard." Then he sweeps me into a big hug and nearly crushes me. "Are you okay?"

He pulls away. Tears prick my eyes when I see the concern in his. I nod, sucking back my tears.

"I'm gonna wring that little punk's neck," my dad says.

"Now Hank, relax. Cam has done enough." Marla places her hand on my dad's arm.

"Cam?" I knew he was mad last night. I called him, but he never answered or came back to the reception. I assumed he never found Derek, that the boat was gone before he could get there, and maybe he needed to blow off some steam.

"He beat up Derek, so now he's with your brother, facing assault charges. What kind of pissant presses charges from a fight after he hit a woman?" Dad shakes his head.

I can read his facial expression. *Another great pick, Chevelle. When are you ever going to learn your lesson?*

"He beat up Derek?"

Okay, I'm not completely surprised. I saw the red veiling Cam's features when he saw my eye. I just hoped the boat would be gone before Cam found Derek so I could calm him down today. Derek isn't worth any of this. I don't want Cam to get into trouble because I chose the wrong guy to date.

"Of course he did," Marla says, as if I was asking if Midge stole the salt and pepper shakers last night. The answer is obviously yes.

"Why do you say it like that?" I ask her.

Marla looks at my dad, and he rolls his eyes and says,

"Don't act dumb, Chevelle. The boy protects you like he's your brother."

"Well..." Marla says.

"Where is he now?" I ask, interrupting their cryptic exchange.

"He's at the sheriff's office."

My doorbell rings before I can tell them I'm heading down there, and my dad opens the door.

Fisher stands on the other side. He shoots me a concerned expression and his gaze traces all over my face, taking me in. "How you doing, sis?"

"I'm okay, just shaken up and embarrassed."

"Hey." He pulls me into a hug. "You have nothing to be embarrassed about. Not at all."

I nod into his chest and suck back tears. Fisher frowns when he pulls away.

"What's going on?" my dad asks.

"I need Chevelle to come down to the station."

"Why?" Marla asks.

"Because you're going to press charges against Derek for assault."

I step back. If I press charges, the entire town will know what happened. I remember the teachers watching me and whispering to each other when I finally went back to school after my mom died. The same thing will happen if people hear about what Derek did to me.

"I think we're all getting ahead of ourselves. Can't we just solve this within the family?" my dad asks.

I'm sure he doesn't want our family name thrown around town again either. It was just as hard for him when Mom died. And then again when Fisher was young and caused all that trouble. Add on when Lucy left Adam. It's like my family can't help but be the center of gossip in town.

"No, we can't, Dad, because Derek has pressed charges on Cam. So now Cam goes to jail unless I have Chevelle press charges on Derek. I'm hoping to lean on Derek when I tell him Chevelle is pressing charges, so he'll drop the ones on Cam. We can drive him out of town and hopefully never see the bastard again." Fisher crosses his arms. He's mad, I can see it in his dark pupils.

"I thought Derek would already be long gone." I worry my lip.

"No such luck." Fisher stands and stares at me, hands on his belt, waiting for me to answer.

"Fine. I'll do it. For Cam."

"We're coming with." Marla puts her hand on my shoulder and escorts me out to Fisher's truck. "Hank, follow us."

My dad does what Marla says because he loves her and he's allowing her to be the mother I don't have. Marla's been a great mother figure, but there really isn't anyone like your own mom. Or maybe that's just me and I should've gone through therapy longer.

We arrive at the sheriff's station and Marla doesn't leave my side as Fisher takes me to his office. Cam is sitting in another room with a soda and candy bar, talking to Mato. Our eyes lock for a moment and he stands, walking toward the door before Mato can stop him.

"I'm fine with the charges, Chevelle," Cam says. "You don't have to do this if you don't want to. No one has to know what happened."

I look at Fisher and back at Cam, then back at Fisher. "Can I talk to him please?"

Fisher sighs and nods.

Mato leaves the room and I walk in, shutting the door. Cam has on one of Fisher's old shirts, a faded threadbare

Sunrise Bay High School Football shirt with his dress slacks. There's a bruise along his cheek, and I notice the way he holds his side when he walks.

"Are you okay?" I ask.

He nods. "Don't worry about me. I'm serious, Chevelle. If you press charges, it'll be reported in the town news. Everyone will know what happened. I know you hate being the gossip in town, so it's fine. Let him come at me. I have witnesses and a lawyer that will get me off."

"Who are your witnesses?" I cross my arms and jut my hip to the side.

"Porter's men were there." He looks outside and leans closer. "They'll tell them that he threw the first punch."

I raise my eyebrows.

"Porter's got three daughters."

I nod. "So Porter and his crew already know?"

He nods again, but there's shame in his eyes. "I had no choice in that. But they're out at sea now."

"Cam, I'm used to people in this town walking on eggshells around me. Now they'll just know I'm a terrible pick when it comes to men too. You didn't have to hit him."

"The hell I didn't. He hurt you."

"You don't have to protect me like my brothers."

He winces but recovers quickly. "I'd hit any slimeball who would hit a woman."

Of course he would. I need to quit thinking of this as one of my romance books where the guy gets all "touch her and die" for the woman he loves. *Get a grip, Chevelle.*

"Regardless, I'm going to get you out of this."

I walk out of the room and into Fisher's office. We file the paperwork even as Cam continues to tell Mato to tell me not to bother. Fisher takes the papers and heads out of the office to the front of the building, where Dad and Marla wait. I follow.

"I want you gone when I get back with him." Fisher looks at my dad to take care of removing me from the station.

"I'll leave when Cam leaves," I say.

Fisher turns around. "No, you won't. You'll leave now. Derek isn't gonna be nice about this, and if I have to scare him and bring him back here to throw him in jail, I don't want you adding fuel to the fire by being here."

"But—"

"Chevelle." He grips the bridge of his nose and glares at his feet before looking back at me. "I'm hanging on by a fucking thread right now. I'm trying to be the sheriff, protect my best friend and you, when what I really want to do is finish what Cam started. He hit my little sister."

Dad looks at me, and I nod in understanding. "I'll be gone."

"Thank you," Fisher mumbles. He pulls me into a quick hug before leaving.

I step back down the hall and take one last look at Cam in the interrogation room. His eyes meet mine, but Marla puts her arm around me and guides me to the door. I hope Fisher's plan works, because I'd hate to be responsible for someone else's future dying.

My dad and Marla take me to their house. We file in through the garage and into the kitchen as the basement door opens. Rylan comes out shirtless with shorts on. He's seventeen now and is practically the size of our older brothers.

"Ry?" Marla asks. "You slept in the basement?"

He glances over his shoulder quickly and I raise my eyebrows when I spot a brunette tucked behind his back.

"Um... yeah. I... uh... fell asleep."

Marla continues into the kitchen, obviously missing the girl I can see from my angle. Dad's already at the fridge, talking about what to make me for breakfast.

"Don't forget you have soccer this morning," Marla calls to Rylan.

I'm standing in the hallway, waiting to see who the girl is, but Rylan's acting as though I can't see her. I decide to do my half brother a solid and step into the little nook in the kitchen where the keys are kept and grab his. I toss them to him. "Here you go."

"Thanks," he says with relief.

I nod and keep my eye on our parents while he grabs the hand of the brunette wearing his shirt and a skirt. It's all I can do not to react, because it's Calista Bailey he's holding hands with. He ushers her down the hallway of the laundry room, stops to grab a bag, and they both exit the house. He mouths *thank you* to me as the door shuts behind him.

"Did he leave already?" Marla peeks over my shoulder. "He probably didn't even brush his teeth or anything."

"He took his bag from the laundry room. You keep spares in there for long tournaments, right?"

She smiles and turns back to the kitchen. "I do. Not sure how that boy will survive next year in college."

Rylan got a full-ride scholarship to Stanford to play soccer. I thought he and Calista were sort of rivals, but I guess something has changed. It's going to be hard not telling the rest of our siblings, since there are bets going around that they'll end up together.

My dad makes me breakfast—Mickey Mouse pancakes like he used to when we were little and having a rough morning. He made them for me the day after my mom died and again on the day of her funeral and pretty much every day for the entire first year after her death.

Marla pats my hand when Dad leaves to go to the bathroom. "He thinks he's helping."

"I know." And I do. My dad means well, but this all reminds me of the last time I felt responsible for something. Not that it's my fault Derek the douche hit me, but I gave him a second chance, didn't I?

The phone rings an hour later. It's Fisher, so my dad puts it on speaker.

"Derek dropped the charges on Cam, so we'll drop Chevelle's charges on Derek. He promised me he'd leave the area for good this afternoon, but we can't force him to leave town. Hopefully he really does leave."

"All good news," my dad says.

Fisher sighs. "Except Cam is homeless. His dad kicked him out of his apartment and took away the keys to his car."

My stomach sinks. Cam would never be in this predicament if it weren't for me.

Dad and Marla look at me.

"What?"

"You have an entire house to yourself now that Mandi and Noah have bought the place next to the inn," Dad says.

"They did?" I had no idea.

He nods. "Noah told me about it last night and asked if they could use my pickup today to start moving their stuff in right away. Think they'll be gone by dinner."

"Mandi didn't mention anything to me." I can't deny that I'm a little hurt she didn't think she could say something.

"Noah bought it as a surprise," my dad says.

I smile and any hurt I had disappears. "That's so sweet."

He shrugs. "I thought so. Now, about where Cam's gonna live..."

"You want Cam to live with me?" I don't think my eyes could get any wider.

"Chevelle's right. We should think this over," Marla says.

"It's your decision, but I'll be honest... I don't like the idea of you living here alone when we don't know for sure what Derek is gonna do. Cam is like family, and he could use some help right now. Besides, your house is close enough to the marina that Cam can walk to work," Dad says.

"I second Dad," Fisher says through the speaker.

Marla raises her eyebrows and bites the inside of her lip.

I can't see Derek making another appearance, but my dad has a point. "Okay, I guess. Cam can move in with me."

"That's my girl," my dad says.

"I'll drop him off later. Until we know for sure this Derek guy is gone, it'll be nice to know Cam's with you to protect you." Fisher hangs up without saying goodbye.

The pit of my stomach sours. How am I going to live with the guy I've crushed on for years without wanting to give in to temptation?

Chapter Seven

Cam

Fisher comes into the interrogation room, sits in the chair across from me, and sighs.

"What? Just tell me."

He looks up and smiles. "Thank your best friend Fisher for bailing you out of trouble again."

I stare at him for a beat. "He caved?"

"Yes. So again... thank your best friend Fisher." He points at himself, his smile wide and annoying as all hell.

"Thanks. Although you could've been nicer when you arrested me. You didn't even let me get a shirt."

He stands and I follow suit. "I can't treat you differently than I would anyone else. People wouldn't vote for me next year." He shrugs.

"I hit somebody to protect the honor of your sister."

I don't miss the way his jaw tightens at the mention of what happened to Chevelle. "I didn't know that. I thought maybe you got drunk and got into a fight."

"Derek was at Mandi's wedding as Chevelle's date. When he pressed charges, what did you think?" I shake my head as we leave the interrogation room. At least he never put me in an actual jail cell. I can just imagine him snapping a few pictures and spreading them around town as a joke.

"Well, I'm a little busy and sleep deprived with, oh that's

right, raising twins. Do you know how hard it's been since they started to crawl? And Allie called this morning after I left to say Laurie has started running. My life is officially over."

I laugh because he's so dramatic. "It's supposed to be a blessing raising kids." I slap him on the shoulder. "Thanks again for springing me. Drive me home?"

He stops short of the door and his eyes crinkle at the sides. He puts his fingers on the bridge of his nose. It's his way of saying there's more he has to tell me. "So, your dad called me because he wanted to know if he should send a lawyer over."

"I knew he wouldn't stay mad at me." I reach for the door.

"I told him we worked it out, and he thanked me and asked if you could stay in the apartment above our garage. He's having a crew box up the stuff from your apartment and he's taking the car back. You've been cut off."

My head rocks back. "I thought for sure he was bluffing."

Fisher shakes his head. "But I found you a better place to stay."

"Better than above your garage? I'm sure I'd find it comfortable there." I shrug.

"Yeah, the apartment is filled with a lot of storage right now. And you know... Allie and the twins—you don't want us to bring down your social life."

"I don't?" He clearly doesn't want me to live with them.

"Chevelle has the entire house to herself, and you can walk to the marina from there. Problem solved. Not to mention, the girls have left all their furniture behind, so bonus for you."

"You want me to live with your sister?"

Hearing him say this is almost like a dream. I thought

for sure Fisher saw right through me and knew I've wanted his sister for a while now, but I guess I was wrong. I'm surprised Chevelle would even agree to it, and I can't help but wonder why she would.

"You're family, Cam." He hits me on the back as he opens the door to the outside. It's still cloudy and foggy, as if the sun decided not to show today. "The only thing I'm worried about is getting calls from the neighbors when you two fight." He laughs and climbs into his sheriff's truck.

I get into the passenger side. "Can you take me to my apartment to get my clothes and stuff?"

"Sure."

As we pull away, I still can't wrap my head around the fact that he set it up for me to move in with Chevelle. This has to be a joke the universe is playing on me. I'm gonna have to see her in her pajamas, and please tell me she's not a tank-top-and-panties girl because I'm going to be living with blue balls until my dad takes me back into the fold.

"Why do you seem stressed? You should be relaxed that you're in the clear." Fisher turns down my street.

"I'm not. It's just… I've never lived with a girl before."

His forehead crinkles when he glances at me as he stops at a stop sign. "It's my sister, man. It's not like it's a girl you're, like, hot for or anything." He laughs, but my stomach sours.

If he only knew.

"Yeah, but still. I'm an only child. I don't want to offend her or anything."

"Chevelle?" He laughs again. "You know her. She'll tell you if you're pissing her off."

Since I have no other options, I sit in his truck, stewing over the fact that I'm going to live with Chevelle. Stupid things can happen when you lust after someone, and the

Greenes are like family to me. Fisher isn't just my best friend, he's like a brother. I cannot fuck this up.

Fisher stops outside my apartment, and sure enough, my dad's Range Rover is parked outside. He's probably dictating to the movers exactly where to move my stuff.

My neighbor's door opens, and my dog, Gunner, runs out to greet us before I make it into my apartment. Chip agreed to watch him overnight since I was expecting to be home late.

"Hey, boy, did Chip treat you well?" I run my hand over his yellow fur. He wags his tail and pants excitedly.

"Since I was nice enough to take him in for the night, I think I deserve to know why you were arrested?" Chip comes out wearing his robe. He's Nikki's sidekick on the morning show of the local radio station and an active participant in Nikki's gossip segment, Scandals of Sunrise Bay. "And now your dad is in there." He nods toward my place next door. "What's up with that?"

"I'm sure Nikki put her own spin on it." Fisher disregards Chip and heads into my apartment.

Gunner follows him because Fisher always gives him too many treats.

"Cameron?" Chip gives me the eye. I do feel bad that Nikki always has the gossip over him. And he's always been good with me when I needed him to watch Gunner for a night.

I step closer and lower my voice. "I hit one of the fishermen and he pressed charges."

"Why?"

"That I can't say. I don't want to bring anyone else into it." Nikki will dig and she'll probably put Chevelle and me out there anyway, but I don't want to be the reason the information is out there. "Believe me, you don't want in first on this story. Hank Greene won't be happy if it gets out."

Chip nods and retreats toward his apartment. "So, you're moving?"

"Being evicted. My dad just cut me off."

His eyes light up because he scored some gossip. Whatever. If the town stays talking about me and not Chevelle, then I'm happy.

I wave goodbye to Chip and walk into my apartment. Sure enough, half my shit is in boxes. I should be furious, but honestly, I don't even care at this point.

"Got out, huh?" my dad says.

"Cam did the right thing, Mr. Baker," Fisher says.

My dad doesn't really see Fisher as the sheriff of our small town because he's the guy who initiated our senior prank of putting a petting zoo in our gym. Not to mention he was the planner of most of our bonfire parties. Let's just say Fisher and I weren't exactly excelling in academics and the sheriff at the time always came to us first when something happened around town.

"It's good now that his sidekick is the sheriff, you can get him off instead of me having to step in." My dad pushes a rolling suitcase my way. "Here are your clothes. There are two more suitcases in the bedroom. Everything else is going into storage."

I shake my head over my dad doing this over me sticking up for a woman.

"With all due respect," Fisher says, but my dad puts up his hand, not wanting to hear another excuse for my behavior.

"No, Fisher."

"He did it because that asswipe hit my sister."

My dad sighs and looks at me. "I heard, and it's

admirable. I'm glad it wasn't a bar brawl, but if you're going to run the marina, you can't be popping off like that. You have to keep your emotions in check. It might not seem like it now, but I'm doing this for your own good. I should've done it when you came back from college."

"It's fine." I shrug, not wanting my dad to see my true irritation.

"Fisher, give us a minute."

Fisher bends down and pets Gunner. "Come on, boy. Let's make sure they didn't pack away all your snacks."

They leave in the direction of the kitchen.

"Listen, Cameron, I understand why you did it. I know you've had a..." He looks in the direction Fisher went. "Thing for the Greene girl, but you can't go around assaulting people. Since the situation wasn't what I thought initially, I'm gonna give you an opportunity—run the fishing boat, get it going, make it a success, and you're back in the fold. You can have your place back, the car, your trust fund, and the marina."

He leaves me no choice but to do what he says. All the money I had in savings is tied up so I can't even use that. Wait until Chevelle finds out I'm starting up a competing business. No way she'll let me stay at her place then. A million scenarios run through my head, other options for a future, but at this juncture, I have no choice if I want to stay in my dad's good graces. And right now, I don't have another option. Not one I know I can count on anyway. I like working at the marina and feeling like part of the community there. I just wish I didn't have to run it the way my dad does.

"Fine, I'll do it." Somehow I manage to keep my voice even.

He gives me the smile I hate, the smug one that signifies

he got his way. "I'll meet you first thing tomorrow morning to go over logistics. The locks to your office have been changed, so meet me at my office." He walks toward the door. "And call your mother. She's worried."

Once he leaves and shuts the door, I plop down on my chair and throw my head in my hands. I still need him and this opportunity. I just hope Chevelle understands.

Fisher comes back into the room. "Allie called and I gotta stop and get diapers and drop them off at the house. Supposedly, I opened the last box and never told her." He rolls his eyes, although he probably did. "I packed Gunner's stuff for you." He holds out a garbage bag.

I mumble thanks as I take the bag, and we leave my apartment that's now full of boxes. In the sheriff's truck, Gunner sandwiches himself on my lap, panting at the window, so I roll it down and he sticks his head out.

Fisher stops at the driveway of where all the Greene girl siblings have lived at one time or another. It's directly across the street from their parents, who look down over town from their house on the big hill.

"I gotta go before Allie blows up my phone again." He takes two of the suitcases, puts them on the doorstep, then shakes my hand and pats me on the back.

"Thanks for getting me off."

He winks. "It's what best friends do."

After he pulls away, I knock on the door.

No answer.

I frown and ring the doorbell.

Gunner sits next to me, his tongue hanging out, waiting patiently for the door to open. He loves Chevelle and has probably picked up her scent already.

I pat his head. "I know. I feel it too." My heart thumps, and there's this weird fluttery feeling in my chest, as if my heart has grown wings. Am I really going to live with Chevelle Greene?

I'm about to ring the doorbell again when the door springs open and Chevelle is standing there with only a towel wrapped around her body.

Fuck me. My dick twitches in my pants.

"Honey, I'm home," I say, trying to get my reaction under control and trying not to think of what she looks like underneath that towel.

She narrows her eyes. "Of course you pick the worst possible time."

My jaw clenches when I clock the bruise on her face again.

Gunner hops up at her and his paws get stuck on the top of her towel.

"Shit." I step forward to help her, but she gets him down without needing me.

"Jeez, your dog is just as horny as you." She turns down the hallway. Jesus, that towel couldn't be any shorter.

Gunner looks up at me. I pet his head.

"I know, the dog park has nothing on her," I mumble and bring my bags into my new place.

God help us all. I already feel the blue balls starting.

Chevelle

That was a mistake. I should have put on a robe or something. Or maybe I should've waited to have a shower until after Cam showed up. But I needed to burn off some anxious energy, so I decided to work out and I hated the thought of him showing up and finding me gross and sweat soaked. Still, it shouldn't matter—he's Fisher's best friend and not at all right for me. I'm playing games with Cam that will only end in disaster.

Now, as I throw on a pair of leggings and a T-shirt and wrap my hair in a towel, I mentally steel myself before I head downstairs.

He's putting out food and water for Gunner. As soon as I land on the bottom step of the stairs, Gunner barrels toward me, his tail wagging nonstop.

"Hey, boy," I say. "Behaving yourself?"

"If you mean has he gotten anyone else knocked up, no. But we were banned from the dog park for humping too many poodles. He's got something for the poodles." Cam leans his big shoulder along the doorframe of the kitchen.

"Just like his dad. Did you train him when he was younger?" I walk past him into the kitchen to grab a water bottle.

Cam doesn't move. "There's nothing wrong with a healthy sexual appetite."

I laugh, shaking my head. "Excuse me."

He holds up his hands and moves out of my way. I go to the fridge and grab a water.

"Let's make some ground rules, Casanova." I sit on a chair at the kitchen table.

"By all means, put more restrictions on me." He joins me at the table but flips the chair around so he's straddling it. Why is that so sexy to me? It's stupid and childish when he could just sit like a normal person.

"First of all, no girls."

He raises his eyebrows. "So, no boys for you?"

Crap, I hadn't really thought about that. I can't forbid him to have girls here and bring guys back here myself. "I don't want to find your girls half-naked in the kitchen."

"Are you suggesting we go this entire time without sex?"

"We'll just go to the other person's house."

He nods. "Fine."

"Really?"

"What?"

"I thought you'd be more difficult." I cross my legs and his gaze dips, tracking the movement.

"It's your house." He shrugs. "I'll pay rent, obviously."

I walk over to grab the spare key from the counter where I left it. "Here's your key. And we only owe my parents rent. It's minimal, and they're so thankful for you sticking up for me that they probably won't even charge you."

"I'll make sure they take my money."

I sit back down and lean back in the chair while he pulls out his keys and puts the house key on the chain. "So, what are you gonna do now? For money?"

He shrugs but sets his gaze on me. Something about the

way he's looking at me... uneasiness coats my insides. I'm definitely missing something.

"What?" I ask.

"My dad came to me about two weeks ago, wanting to start a new business venture. He wanted me to head the operation. I told him to hold off because I didn't wanna do it. But now if I ever want my position at the marina back and to be considered for taking over for him when he retires, I have no choice but to do what he wants."

"Which is?" I screw the cap back on my water then tuck my hands under my thighs, worried about what he's going to say.

"A fishing tourist boat."

I open my mouth to protest, but he holds up his hand.

"I'm gonna make it different than yours, cater to a different clientele. He wants more of a luxury experience for people who aren't serious about fishing. It shouldn't affect you."

I stand, unable to sit any longer. "Seriously? Rowdy's gone for sure then."

"The way I see it, all three of us will offer something different."

I lean against the counter, gripping the edge on either side of my body. "Cam, I've worked for years to grow my clientele and be a trusted fisherwoman who can handle the tours."

"That's why I was putting my dad off, but there's nothing I can do, Chevelle. As of right now, I'm cut off."

I want to be furious with him, but he's in this position because of me. "Why did you do it?" I almost whisper.

He looks at the table. I don't have to explain what I'm talking about. "I told you. You're like a sister to me."

He doesn't look at me when he says it. I'm pretty sure we

both know he's lying. At least, a big part of me is hopeful he is.

"Well, I never said thank you, so thank you." I walk out of the kitchen.

"No more rules?" he calls.

I'm at the bottom of the stairs when I stop to say, "I guess we'll figure it out as it comes. I have to go dry my hair, then I need to go check on my boat and prepare for tomorrow. Take whichever bedroom you want."

I head upstairs with the ominous feeling that living with Cam is either going to be a dream or a complete nightmare.

* * *

LATER THAT DAY, I'm at the marina, cleaning my boat, when a brand-new expensive fishing boat is towed into the harbor. It takes one of the prime slips that only yachts are allowed to go in. It's definitely for more expensive charters—I can't imagine what it cost. The Bakers will probably have servers on the boat. My stomach sinks as I realize there's no way Rowdy or I can compete.

"Who's that?" Speaking of which, Rowdy just returned from a charter. I recognize the two guys walking up the dock as guys who've been coming to him every year around this time.

"You didn't hear it from me, but the Bakers are expanding their business interests."

He frowns. "Fishin' excursions?"

"Bingo."

We watch as they get the new boat into the slip. Working the delivery are a group of guys we all call the Baker Muscle —the same four guys who do all the heavy lifting. Neither Mr. Baker nor Cam is even here to see it being delivered.

"More competition. Great," Rowdy says. "I barely made rent last month and somehow my bill hasn't come for this month. Did you get yours?"

My forehead wrinkles. "Yeah, last week. That's weird that you didn't."

"I know. It's almost as if someone paid my bill, but unless I got some fairy godmother I don't know about, that's impossible. They'll probably double bill me next month, really put me out of business."

Rowdy used to be the only one doing fishing charters. I felt bad when I started Reelaxing Fishing Tours, but we cater to different clientele. He has a long list of customers and takes out groups no bigger than four. My boat is bigger and I can go up to ten, so I usually handle the bigger parties. I suppose Rowdy is the small, I'm the medium, and now Cam will be the large.

"What do you know about it?" He nods toward the new boat.

"Cam's heading it up."

He stares at me for a beat. "I heard somethin' about a scuffle on Porter's boat last night..."

I nod. It doesn't matter. By tomorrow, everyone will know that Cameron Baker beat up a guy because of me, but I'm not going to be the one who spreads that news. Besides, the bruise on my face is clearly visible, even with the foundation I put on before I came down here.

"I always found it so interestin'," Rowdy says, both of us watching our competition being placed in the prime spot in the marina.

"What?"

"How the apple fell so far from the tree."

I laugh because that is so Rowdy, saying something odd that needs explanation. "What do you mean?"

"Cam isn't anythin' like his family. He's always down here, talkin' to us, not up there lookin' down on us." He nods toward the building. "He looks out for us and..." He looks me up and down. "Protects us."

I scratch my neck and turn away from his piercing eyes. So, he knows. Great.

Rowdy is right though. Mr. Baker never walks the docks. The Baker Muscle does all his work for him, whereas Cam is down here with us in the trenches. Hearing the stories, making sure everyone makes it back to port, lending a hand when someone needs it.

As they finish with the boat, Vinny, another captain, walks down the pier and stops to see what we're looking at.

"Heard a rumor about the Bakers starting a new venture." He looks at me. "You good, Chevelle?"

I nod. "Fine."

"Glad to hear it." He admires the new boat that will be a permanent fixture here. It's definitely the odd boat out and looks as though it belongs down in California somewhere, not Alaska. "Man, I just got in off the water. Have either of you seen that Five Seas boat?"

"One with the purple stripe?" Rowdy asks. "It's a beaut."

I frown. "I haven't seen it. I've never heard of that boat company."

"I heard it's new, out of Winterberry Falls or something. You'll know it when you see it. They are some gorgeous boats," Vinny says.

"Fishing charters?" I ask Vinny.

He shakes his head. "No, they're like classic wooden boats."

"I'll have to keep my eye out."

"Like I said, you'll know it when you see them." He chuckles.

My eyes catch a familiar figure walking down from the entrance of the marina, a four-legged companion following. Cam glances in our direction and lowers his head, walking to the new boat. He shakes hands with all four of the Baker Muscle, and they hand him a pouch full of stuff. He climbs aboard his new boat with Gunner hopping on right next to him. That dog has been around boats his entire life.

"Lucky bastard," Vinny mumbles. "Anyway, see you guys later." He heads into the warehouse.

"Me too. Gotta hose down, fuel up, and get ready for an early mornin' excursion." Rowdy steps away but turns back, looking at the sky. "Get home 'fore it's dark, okay?"

I chuckle because it's Alaska in the summer. It won't be dark for a long time yet. "Okay, dad." I salute him and he gives a stern expression. "I will, Rowdy. Promise."

He nods. "Good."

Sometimes I think everyone still watches out for me because in their eyes, I'm the little girl who lost her mother.

Cam walks out from the wheelhouse and sits on one of the luxury chairs in the back, staring out at the bay. I try not to watch him as I finish my work, but I can't take my eyes off of him. Gunner sits next to him, and Cam pets his head, not taking his eyes off the horizon.

I wonder what it must be like to have everything handed to you your entire life only for it to be stripped away so fast. I always envied him for having money and going on trips, but I sense that maybe his life isn't as easy as I always thought.

I grab two beers from my fridge and walk down the pier to his boat. "May I come aboard?"

He blinks out of his thoughts, and a smile that weakens my knees shines on his face. "Always."

I try not to read into that and step aboard. Gunner

rushes to me, wanting to kiss my face as I hold out a beer to Cam.

"Welcome to the family." I sit in the chair next to his.

He accepts the beer and cracks it open. "Thanks. Although I thought I was already part of the family."

We clink bottles. "Now you're one of us. Instead of a stuffy, uptight executive."

He chuckles and tips back his bottle. "Guess I need a new wardrobe."

"Yeah, not a lot of captains in suits and polo shirts."

He continues to watch the last of the fishing boats returning to the marina. A woman rushes down the pier toward a boat that I know was out for gold crab. Cam smiles as she waves to a man who barely steps off the boat before she attaches herself to him.

"I can't imagine what that's like," Cam says.

"To be gone that long so often? I don't know how they do it."

He looks at me, expression serious. "No, I mean, I can't imagine having someone miss you that much."

It's the first time I've seen Cam so vulnerable, and I understand what he's saying.

Gunner comes and lies between us. We watch a few more women walk down the docks, some with kids in tow. Each family reunion makes me wonder what it would be like to have someone permanent in my life.

"But you forget the long nights of wondering if they're alive... the fear of losing your loved one always in the back of your head and the knowledge of how common it is. Is all that fear worth the love?" I ask.

He looks at me and I swear he frowns. There I go disappointing someone else again.

Cam

*T*hurry up and finish getting ready since there's only one bathroom in this house. How in the hell did four women live here with only one bathroom?

Gunner lies on the back porch while I prepare breakfast, listening to the sounds of Chevelle getting ready upstairs. There's a lot of cursing and banging, but I ignore it.

Twenty minutes later she comes down, her hair in two braids, a tank top with the name of her company across her breasts and shorts that make me want to bite my knuckles. Especially when she bends over in the fridge to pack her cooler.

"Good morning. Hungry?"

She glances back at me. "You left the floor in the bathroom all wet and I almost fell on my ass."

"Well, I made you breakfast to make up for it." I shrug.

She grabs the Tupperware containers she prepared last night and leans her back against the fridge. "You're being sweet. What's up, Cam? We don't do that."

"You let me move in."

"And you beat a guy up for me. We're even."

I frown at the mention of Derek. "Speaking of, how are you feeling—"

She holds up her hand to stop me. "I'm fine."

I stare at her for a beat.

"I mean it, I am. I just had that one encounter and thankfully I'm out of that situation. I can't imagine what women in abusive relationships go through." She shakes her head, her forehead wrinkled.

"Are you sure?"

"I said I'm fine, Cam."

"But if you needed to talk to someone—"

"I would. But honestly, I'm just glad it's behind me."

I nod then look at the eggs and bacon I've prepared, hoping she's being truthful. "I already made too much, so this is your one chance to have my specialty breakfast."

She accepts my change of subject and chuckles while zipping up her cooler and setting it on the table. "Is this what you make for all your morning-after girls?"

I plate our food on two plates, and she fills a to-go coffee mug.

"You assume I let them stay for breakfast."

She shakes her head. "You're such a pig."

I place the plate in front of her and sit in the chair across from her. My knees almost brush hers under the small round table.

"Gunner sure is comfortable here."

I follow her line of vision to the back porch where he's soaking up the sun on his side. "Yeah, I worried he'd have accidents or something in the house since it's new to him, but he loves it here. Probably 'cause he loves you."

She smiles, and Jesus, what a smile. "He's a great dog."

"The one good thing I've done in my life."

Her toes push at mine under the table. "Stop that. You're going to make a success of your new venture while not putting my business under, right? You'll prove to your dad you deserve to own the marina."

I nod because I haven't told anyone that I'm not even sure that's something I want to do. Most fishermen at the marina don't like or respect my dad. He controls so much and takes away so much of their profits when he buys their catches wholesale and distributes them. I've never wanted to be a cutthroat businessman, but now in my thirties, it feels like it's too late to go back to school. I've pissed away so many years, only caring about the money and the expectation of living up to what my dad wanted for me. And partying. There was a lot of partying.

"I smell something burning. You thinking hard over there?" Chevelle's voice takes me out of my thoughts.

I fork my eggs. "Nothing, just how I'm starting this business from scratch."

She rests her foot on the edge of her chair and wraps her arm around her leg. Her leg looks smooth and sun kissed, and I want to run my hand down it like some sick fuck with a fetish.

"I'll figure it out. I always do." I shrug.

She blinks and gets back to eating her breakfast. "Of course you will."

The last thing I want is for Chevelle to feel sorry for me when she's the one who went through such a huge ordeal with Derek.

"How are you really?" I broach the subject again, thinking maybe she'll be more open now that I've opened up a bit.

She rises from the chair and takes her plate to the sink, rinses it, and puts it in the dishwasher. "Fine. Why?"

"I mean from Mandi's wedding. Chevelle, if you need to talk to someone..." I finish my own meal and meet her at the sink.

"I told you, I'm fine. I just always seem to pick jerks." She walks to the other side of the room and picks up her cooler. "Do you want a ride or are you going to walk?"

"I'll take a ride as long as you don't mind Gunner coming along too."

Hearing his name through the screen door, he perks up and whines at the back door.

"Are you kidding? He's more welcome than you." She lets him in, and they head to the front door.

Chevelle has always prided herself on keeping her emotions to herself. There were years of therapy after her mom's accident, and Fisher would tell me about the nightmares she endured. How no one could convince her not to blame herself for what had happened. And I know that still to this day, the guilt is there inside her, along with the grief. I wish I could unleash her from the pain, but I have no idea how.

I head out of the house, locking it behind me. Gunner is in the front seat.

Chevelle rolls down the window. "Gunner called shotgun."

"Like hell. Get in the back."

Gunner tucks his tail and walks through the center of the two seats and lies down in the back.

"So bossy." She shakes her head.

"You should see me in bed." The statement comes out naturally and I'm not imagining the way her cheeks redden.

I think someone might be thinking about me bossing her around in bed. Good. Because it's pretty much all I've been thinking about since I moved in, and I can't help but feel like we're reaching a breaking point.

A TEXT from my dad on the way over tells me he has three-day charters booked for this weekend. What happened to me getting the business and starting it from scratch? He just can't find it in himself to trust me.

We arrive at the marina, and instead of heading to the air-conditioned offices, I'm heading to a luxury fishing boat.

"Have a good day." Chevelle smiles, continuing to her own boat. "Must be someone important to get that slip." She glances over her shoulder at my new boat.

"I have demons in high places."

She laughs.

Gunner follows her until I whistle, and he returns back to me. We board the boat, and in the wheelhouse, I turn on my computer. I need a name, a social media presence, and a logo. I take out a pad of paper and make a to-do list.

For the majority of the day, I hammer out the details of what I need in order to be out from under my dad's thumb. It's about time I do something for myself. Who would've thought the best thing I could've done for myself was knock out Derek Latrell?

I decide to take a break, walk the docks, and take Gunner to the grass along the side to do his business. Chevelle returns with what I'm surprised to find is a group of three women. She's laughing with them as they dock.

"Oh, do you ever have some eye candy out here," one of them says.

"That's just my brother's best friend," Chevelle says.

I'm oddly offended by Chevelle's remark but happy that her clients like what they see.

"And he's got a dog." Another woman whistles like I do.

Gunner stops, his eyes fly up, and he runs off in the direction of the noise.

"Gunner!" I yell, but it's too late. He's already waiting patiently for Chevelle to tie the boat up.

When she finishes, she calls him over and pets him, nuzzling his face. "This, ladies, is Gunner Baker, the cutest yellow lab you'll ever know."

"Come here, Gunner," the whistling woman calls.

He jumps into Chevelle's boat and licks the woman's face, allowing her to smother him.

"He's as cute as his owner," the other one says.

The three ladies are probably in their early forties. All attractive and outdoorsy types. You can tell by how comfortable they seem on the boat that this isn't their first fishing charter.

"Tell us, where do we find more guys like you?" the third one says, redoing her red hair in a ponytail.

"At any of the local bars," Chevelle says, stepping off the boat and putting her hand on my shoulder as if she's offering me up. "You'll probably see him in the flesh at one of them."

The women's gazes roam up and down my body. "That would be nice. It is a girls' trip."

"Where else are you ladies going?" I ask because they're tourists and flirting with tourists brings them back to our small town, which is always good for the local economy.

"We're hiking tomorrow. You don't happen to be a guide, do you? The guy we talked to had that same deep voice."

"Sorry, ladies, if I took you hiking, I'd probably get you lost and eaten by a bear. My bet is that Denver Bailey is taking you. Great guide. You'll have a lot of fun."

Gunner makes his way around each of the ladies. Chevelle hops back on board her boat and finishes collecting all their stuff.

"So, are you cooking these for dinner?" Chevelle asks,

holding up the fish they caught. "If you go through those doors at the inn"—she points at Mandi's Sunbay Inn—"there are people who will help you turn these into filets, and there are recipe cards with some seasonings you can buy. They'll even wrap and freeze any extras for you to take home with you."

The eyes of the one with the wedding ring gleam. "Oh, that's so fun."

The other two groan. "We're going to stay in this town forever."

"Well, the eye candy in there might be even nicer than the one right in front of you." Chevelle smiles at me.

"Was that a compliment?" I ask.

"For Gunner, yeah." She puts her face into his neck and nuzzles him. "He's great eye candy."

We both look up and all three women are staring at us.

"You two are cute," the red-haired one says. "You could've told us if we were stepping on your toes." She steps out of the boat and onto the pier.

"Brother's best friend, remember?" Chevelle thumbs in my direction.

"We heard you," the one says. "My first crush was my brother's best friend." The one woman continues to look me up and down. I'm not sure she'd care if Chevelle said I was hers.

"Anyway, ladies..." Chevelle passes them their bags and fish. "It was a pleasure having you aboard, and I hope you visit us again soon."

"You're the best ever. We're going to tell all of our friends, but not my husband," the married one says. "You're too gorgeous to be in a boat with my husband for two hours."

"Oh, Jen, please. Look who she has to admire all day." The brunette gestures at me. "She wouldn't want Matt."

Chevelle laughs. "Go so you can shower and enjoy dinner. If you eat at the inn while you're in town, tell them Mandi's sister sent you and you'll probably get a free dessert."

The three women all giggle as they walk down the pier.

"I feel objectified." I hand her the hose from the dock and turn on the water.

She starts spraying down the boat. "It's about time you feel the way I do all day. Now that you're a captain, you better get used to it."

I help Chevelle clean her boat because I don't have much else to do.

After we're finished, Rowdy wanders over. "So, you're goin' into our business, huh?"

I nod. "Appears so."

"Well, I was thinkin' about how to make you feel like one of us, so here yah go." He tosses a bag at me, and I catch it.

Opening the bag, I see the fish costume I've sometimes seen people wearing at the entrance to the marina when they're trying to sell the fishing tours. "And?"

"Need to earn your spot, so you have to wear it."

"I'm not wearing it." I hold the bag out in his direction, but he doesn't take it.

Chevelle high-fives Rowdy. "Love it."

I set the bag on the deck. "How about a bet to see who has to wear it instead?"

No way Chevelle will back down, but I can see Rowdy throwing around his longtime status as a reason he shouldn't have to wear the costume.

"Okay, whoever has the least pounds of fish caught after this month wears the costume for an afternoon." Rowdy knows he's going to win. He knows all the hot fishing spots.

I'm pretty sure the people my dad booked are probably

coming aboard strictly for entertainment and not for catching fish. But I won't turn down the bet even if I have to wear the costume. "I'm in."

We all shake hands.

"Oh, this is going to be fun. I can't wait." Chevelle waves at her next charter, a foursome of men heading toward us. "Beat it, boys, my next charter is here."

I growl even though they're older and step out of the boat as the men approach. Rowdy heads over to his boat.

"Nice to meet you. I'm Cameron Baker, the owner of the marina. We're happy you came to enjoy a day of fishing. My girlfriend, Chevelle, knows all the great spots." I wave in her direction and Chevelle's jaw drops. "I'll see you out there, honey." I look at all the men. "I have my own charter, so you never know when I could just pop up."

The men get the hint quickly to not try anything with Chevelle.

"Bye, sweetie." Chevelle pushes me when they all turn their backs to get on the boat.

I laugh and whistle for Gunner, who follows obediently. Chevelle flips me off as she starts the boat and steers it toward the bay. God, I love seeing her riled up. One day that's gonna bite me in the ass.

Chapter Ten

Chevelle

This bet has gotten my competitive juices flowing. I wore that fish costume all the time when I started out and it smells disgusting, which I'm pretty sure Rowdy did on purpose. I almost threw up every day and would hide behind buildings just to take it off and get some fresh air for a bit. And when I'd get home, my sisters would complain about how much I smelled and tell me to take a shower, when I'd already showered and scrubbed myself clean. So there is no way I'm losing this bet.

The problem is, Rowdy is ancient and knows every fishing corner in the area. And Cam's supernova boat probably has killer radar that will take him directly to the fish. Which means if I don't use some stealthy planning, my ass will be in that suit.

Friday morning, the first day of our competition, I have the morning off since I don't have a charter booked. Most weekenders drive in on Friday morning and book for Friday afternoon or Saturday. But I saw on the log that Cam has an excursion booked with six guys.

He hasn't shown up yet and was still in the shower when I left. The docks are quiet since most of the fishermen are still out for the week. Rowdy took his first charter out because his clientele leans toward older people who are usually up at the butt crack of dawn anyway.

Since no one is around, I lean down on the dock and grab a fish floating on the water. Whether he slipped off a boat or just floated to shore, he's definitely dead.

I pick it up with both hands and smell it, my face jerking back. Cam's clients are definitely not going to have the great charter they were promised. Looking around again, I'm surprised it's so quiet out here. I step onto his new boat.

Getting to really look around this time, I realize it's nicer than I thought. And bingo—he's got radar. I need an edge, so I toss Mr. Smelly Fish under one of the bench seats with the life preservers. Hopefully it stays in the sunlight all day and bakes away.

"Gunner!"

Cam's voice makes me bolt up then hunker down. He's coming this way, and I have no excuse for being on his boat. And Gunner will scent me out in no time.

I head down to the little galley because the boat is posh and of course he has a place for people to chill and get out of the sun or cold. There's a bedroom and a little sitting area. He's got a notepad with notes scribbled in his handwriting. I can't really decipher any of it. I look through one of the small windows and see Cam come aboard with two cases of beer. His head is cranked to the side, holding his phone between his shoulder and cheek.

"I told you I needed that by this weekend. Has to be the same color," he says.

The person on the other end must say something.

"They're expecting it Monday when they get into town. Do I have to remind you that this is a company and I'm not going to start pissing off customers? Get me the same color or I'll find someone else." He sets down the beer and hangs up his cell phone. "Some people, Gunner. Be happy all you have to do all day is flirt, sleep, and shit."

Gunner whines.

"I know, if you could just go back to the dog park, right? It was like your own little strip club."

I bite my lip to keep from laughing. Cam loves his dog. Makes me think he'll be a good dad one day.

God, where the hell did that thought come from?

He heads back off the boat and my assumption is he must need more supplies. I sneak back up to the wheel-house and peek through the window. But a nose moves between my thighs and lifts into my ass. I reach behind me and get a handful of fur.

Gunner.

I quickly turn and Gunner pounces his front paws on me, making me lose my balance. I screech as I plop down on my ass.

"Ugh... Gunner," I seethe through my teeth.

"What are you doing on my boat?" Cam asks, now standing in the wheelhouse doorway.

"Nothing." I get up and brush off my ass. "Bad boy, Gunner. Friends keep secrets." I pet him so he knows I don't really mean it.

"Bullshit. You trying to poison my guests, or find out where I'm taking them so you can get there first?"

"No." I give him the most innocent look I can muster.

He narrows his eyes. "What do you think? Want to partner up against Rowdy?"

"No, that's not fair." I move to leave the galley, but he blocks my way.

"I should make you pay money to see the boat."

I put my hands in my pockets. "I don't have any money, sorry."

"Then maybe a kiss?"

"Oh yeah, because I'm your girlfriend? Those guys were old enough to be my dad. You didn't have to try to scare them."

"Why, did they hit on you?"

"You know, Cam, some men take me seriously as their fishing tour guide. You might only see tits and ass, but other people see a competent woman." I push him away and make my way off the boat onto the dock.

"Oh, come on, Chevelle, you know that's not what I see…" He continues carrying on while I walk over to my boat.

That should stop him from trying to figure out why I was on his boat in the first place. I smile the entire time I walk away.

I'M in my bikini and my bright-orange fishing overalls, cleaning my boat and getting ready for my first charter of the day. I might not have had a charter this morning, but I waved goodbye to Cam as I lay in my boat wearing my bikini.

He had to bite his tongue when he usually would've yelled at me to put on some clothes.

I'm wiping down the seats when Cam's boat pulls into the marina. Everyone on the boat is green and sitting on the benches. The smell may have dissipated if they threw the fish overboard, but I'm sure it's burned into their nostrils. The fishing poles don't look like they got much use.

"Chevelle, you better stay right there," he squawks over the radio.

I look up with a confused expression.

"Don't play coy. We all know what you did."

He docks the boat and I hate how good he is at maneuvering such a big boat. It's kind of a turn-on. And then I have to watch his muscles bulge as he throws out the lines to someone on the dock. The man is way too sexy for his own good.

I leave my boat, still in my overalls, hoping the small glimpse of skin will make him tongue-tied. Or at least it should.

"I'm very sorry about this. I'll refund your money and do a complimentary booking," he tells the group, but they all ignore him, walking down the dock.

"Didn't catch anything?" I ask with a saccharine sweet voice.

He comes down off the boat. "You put that fish in there, didn't you?"

I shake my head, crossing my fingers behind my back. "I don't know what you're talking about."

He grabs my arm and pulls it out as I quickly undo my fingers. "You're still lying. Crossing your fingers doesn't work."

I shrug again at my last failed attempt to feign innocence.

"I'll give you props though. I didn't even realize it until we stopped to fish and they mentioned the smell. Bravo." He leans forward. "Payback will be a bitch though."

I laugh. "Try it. But right now, my charter is coming, so I better change. I don't want them getting the wrong idea."

I unclip my overalls and allow them to drop to the ground. Cam watches me with a heated glare as I step out of the overalls and turn around to walk back to my boat.

Right before I turn down my own pier, I glance over my shoulder. "You did say payback was a bitch, right?"

He opens his mouth but shuts it.

"Thought so."

Then I catch sight of some familiar people over his shoulder, and I don't like it. It's a group of elderly people, and my grandma leads the pack.

"Cameron!" Ethel raises her arm.

You've got to be kidding me. I turn back around and stomp over to them, which loses some of its effectiveness since I'm in a bikini.

"Grandma!" I shout, and she touches her ear.

"Don't yell, dear. How are you, sweetheart?" She inspects my face, and I'm instantly reminded of the fact everyone knows about Derek. Luckily, the bruise is mostly gone now.

I lower her arm. "I'm fine. Why are you looking for Cam?"

She signals to the group she's with. "We booked him for a charter. New business."

"Yes, but your granddaughter already does fishing charters." I keep my voice low.

"And I booked a charter with you when you first started, remember?" She pats my cheek.

How can I forget? She and Dori asked me to take them to party island because they'd heard rumors of it and wanted to see what it was about. I did, and they actually partied with the kids who were about forty years younger than them. Never underestimate my grandma.

"Yes, but Cam is my competition."

"Not competition. There's enough business for everyone." She runs her hand down my arm. "It's Earl's birthday and we wanted to do something fun."

"I could've taken you out."

She looks past me, and my shoulders sag a bit, knowing my boat doesn't compare to Cam's. "Next time, dear. We need the cushions for our butts. You understand."

"Uh-huh."

She walks back over to her group. Cam winks at me over their heads and I roll my eyes.

"Okay, ladies and gentlemen, I just need to refuel, grab a few more bottles of water, do a little disinfecting"—he glares over at me—"and then we'll be on our way. I apologize for the delay. I got a little distracted."

Earl and Isaac look my way. "I would too."

Ew… I turn toward my boat to go change.

Cam escorts them all onto his boat and serves them food and drinks. I bet none of them will fish, so he's screwed as far as the bet goes anyway.

In the wheelhouse of my boat, I quickly change into shorts and a T-shirt. By the time I come out, my charter guests are walking down the pier. They're four men who look like serious fishermen and are maybe a few years older than me. They're good-looking and I'm kind of wishing I kept the bikini on.

"Welcome," I say.

"You're Chevelle, right?" the guy I'm assuming booked me, whose name is Jack, says. "Next time can we get on your boyfriend's boat? That's one nice fishing vessel."

All four men turn toward Cam's boat. He salutes me as he's backing up to head out to the open seas.

"Oh, he's not my boyfriend."

"He told us that you like to keep it secret since you work so closely together. Don't worry, your secret is safe with us." Jack winks.

I blow out a frustrated breath.

Just before Cam leaves, he honks the horn of the boat and winks. "See you soon. Miss you every minute."

"He seems like a cool guy," one of the guys says.

"Everyone sit down so I can cover the safety stuff, then we'll be on our way."

I could kill Cam, but then again, I guess payback is what I deserve. At least it didn't threaten my catch. It could've been worse. But he has to stop telling people he's my boyfriend like some jealous lover. Or maybe that's wishful thinking. Maybe he's just acting like an overprotective brother.

Cam

I've finished a week's worth of charters, and it hasn't been that bad after the fish incident. I have my own plans to mess up one of Chevelle's, but I need to do it when she least expects it. Telling every group of guys that hires her that I'm her boyfriend might keep them from hitting on her, but it doesn't keep her from winning the bet.

Rowdy only does small groups, but he could easily come in first or second just because of the consistency of his business, but Chevelle takes out more clients.

I'm in the shower, thinking about all of this as water washes down my body. I'm trying to keep my mind occupied because it keeps wandering to Chevelle and that damn bikini she wore with the orange overalls. I've already jerked off to the fantasy of stripping it all off her every damn night this week and still my dick isn't satisfied. Just the thought of her naked under those water-logger overalls, my hand sliding through the opening, grabbing her breast, tweaking her nipple makes my heart rate pick up.

"Fuck," I murmur, having no choice but to get myself off again.

With one hand against the tile wall, my free hand grabs my dick, pumping my half chub until it grows long and hard. Images flash in my mind of unclipping one of the buttons on the overalls, the orange flap falling down and exposing her tit. Her wanton eyes on me, begging me to worship her body.

I bend down and take a nipple into my mouth, swirling my tongue around her hard bud while my hand moves to the other side and allows the overalls to fall down to her ankles, exposing her completely. I step back and soak in the body I've been dying to see naked since I got a sneak peek of it when she had to stay in my room during the family Hawaii vacation. In my mind, she's not embarrassed, because that's not really her style. She owns her body. It's one thing I absolutely love about her.

"Well, are you just going to stare?" she asks me in my mind.

"Fuck no," I say.

I grab her around the waist and my lips smash against hers. Our tongues tangle and I grow harder in my hand.

She grabs my clothes and I help her, shedding my T-shirt and shorts. Her gaze falls to my dick pointing north and her tongue slides out of her mouth, licking her lips. The sexiest thing I've ever seen is when she falls to her knees and takes me in her hand.

Shit. Shit. Shit. I worry I won't be able to hold my orgasm back until I'm inside her.

She wraps her hand around my base and inches forward, never breaking eye contact with me, sliding her tongue up my shaft. My hand winds through her blonde hair and I make a fist in her hair, but I don't guide her or force her, because Chevelle isn't the type to go for that. She's going to want to control this situation and I'm more than willing to let her.

I plunge forward when her mouth encases the top of my dick. Instantly my balls pull up and my orgasm is right there, wanting to finish in her mouth. For a moment, I wonder if she's a spit or swallow girl, but then she deep throats me.

"Fuck, Chevelle." I moan, and she slowly withdraws me from her mouth before encasing me again.

She continues the deep-throat action and slowly pulls back, her tongue doing magical things I've never experienced before, all while she pumps me with her hand. I struggle not to grab her face and fuck her mouth. Her pace increases, and I'm right there, ready to blow.

My bicep is flexed, the muscles in my forearm corded as I jerk back and forth on my cock, ready to finish this fantasy in the shower. All I see are her big eyes staring up at me, filled with lust and hunger. I'm gonna come. Shit. Here it—

The bathroom door flies open, the toilet lid smacks the back of the toilet, and a woman sighs.

My hand instantly stills on my dick and I stand straight to peek around the curtain to see Chevelle sitting on the toilet. I pop back behind the curtain.

"Chevelle!" I shout because what the fuck? I was right there, and my dick is so hard it's painful.

"I'm sorry, but you were taking too long. I had to pee."

Yet another reason there needs to be another bathroom in this damn house.

"I was busy," I grind out.

"Oh please, Cam, you don't have anything I haven't seen."

"But—"

"I'm not a guy. I can't just whip it out and go wherever."

I hear her grab the toilet paper and I watch my dick deflate as the blue ball ache sets into my nuts. She flushes and the water turns cold for an instant. I jump to the other side of the tub.

"You'd be pissed if I walked in on you."

"I don't take as long of showers as you. Seriously, what are you doing in there?" She moves to the sink and washes her hands.

"I'm showering so I smell good."

"What, do you have a date tonight?" Do I detect a note of... something in her voice?

"No."

She moves to dry her hands. I cannot believe she's staying here this long.

"Oh... wait, I get it now. You have a bedroom, Cam. Don't waste all the warm water on that. I have to shower too."

A visual of us sharing a shower assaults me. Usually I'd say some smart-ass comment, but right now I want her out of this bathroom. "It's not what you think."

"That's what Adam used to say... but you weren't, like, doing it when I walked in, were you?"

"Chevelle, get the hell out of the bathroom!"

"Oh my god, you were? Ew, and now I have to shower after you."

"Get out!"

"Now that I have you in a situation where you can't leave unless you want me to see you naked..." I peek around the curtain and see her prop herself up on the counter. "Telling my customers you're my boyfriend has to stop."

I grin. "Why, when it works so well?"

"It's pissing me off."

I get back under the showerhead and wash my hair. "That's the point."

"It makes my charters think I can't handle myself out there. Stop doing it."

"But it's okay for you to put a dead fish in my boat?"

She laughs. "Okay, I'm sorry for that. Kind of."

I finish showering and turn off the water, grabbing my towel from the rack and drying myself behind the curtain. "It's now or never, Chevelle. Leave the bathroom."

"There you go, always bossing me around." I hear her hop down from the counter.

I purposely open the curtain, towel wrapped around my waist. Now that junior has calmed down, he's not sticking out of the opening.

She covers her eyes. "I was leaving."

I step out of the shower. "Don't leave on my account."

I love playing games with her. She scrambles for the door with her hand over her eyes.

"Seriously though, don't finish in the bathtub. I take baths in there." She opens the door.

"It goes down the drain."

"Ew!" A full-body shiver racks her.

I put my hand on the door to keep it shut and lean into her. She turns and her back falls against the door. She stares up at me, the humor in the small space dissipating, replaced by heady lust.

God, I want her so fucking bad.

"Next time, don't come into the bathroom until I'm done."

She glances down. "Done doing what?"

"Do you really want me to tell you?"

I see the challenge in her eyes. She wants me to say it and a big part of me wants to tell her. Maybe if I do, the visual from moments before will come true.

I lean in closer, my mouth inches from her ear, and she doesn't pull back. "Do you want to know who and what I was imagining?"

Her breath hitches and I step in even closer, our bodies about to touch.

"What's your answer, Chevelle?" I whisper, my breath blowing in her ear.

She squirms, and I'd bet money her nipples are peaked. I know I'm hyperaware of her being so close to me.

All the reasons I can't touch her run through my mind. Fisher, my best friend who is trusting me to live with his little sister. The fact that her family is like my own family at this point and if I ever hurt Chevelle, I'd do irreparable damage to my relationships with the rest of the Greenes. And the fact that I don't think either of us is looking for anything serious.

I draw back from her ear and my eyes fix on her lips. Her tongue slides out and coats her plump lips. She wants this just like I do. She's inches away and all I want is to feel her tits smash into my naked chest and feel her lips on mine.

"Hello?" Fisher's voice sounds from downstairs.

Chevelle pushes me away with both hands.

Since I'm not prepared, I fall back. My ass hits the counter as she flees from the room, slamming the door. I look down at where junior is poking out of the towel now.

"Damn, that was almost our chance. Fucking Fisher." Though in truth, I should be thanking him for preventing me from doing something stupid.

I shake my head. Imagine he caught us fucking? I'd probably be dragged down the steps by my hair and buried alive. I might be Fisher's best friend and he trusts me with a lot of shit, but I'm not sure his baby sister is one of them. We just did too much fucking around back in the day for him to ever think I could settle down with one woman. For him not to picture me doing the same kind of things with his baby sister.

I open the door and go to my room, where I shove on a

pair of basketball shorts and a T-shirt before heading downstairs.

They're in the living room. Chevelle is on the chair with her legs crossed, and Fisher is on the edge of the couch.

"What's up, man?" I fist-bump him and join him on the couch.

It's still weird to see my best friend, my delinquent teenage sidekick, in a role of authority. He was the biggest rule breaker when we were growing up. Now he's dressed like the guys we used to run from.

"I was just telling Chevelle that Derek has left town. I got a call from a police station in Washington asking about the charges that were dropped. I guess he got pulled over for drunk driving. Needless to say, I doubt he'll come back here again."

I look at Chevelle. "That's good news."

"Definitely." She rises off the chair. "Thanks, Fish." She leans down and kisses his cheek. "I'm going to go shower."

She walks up the stairs, and it takes every ounce of effort not to follow her.

"How you enjoying it here?" Fisher asks. "I was thinking... if you guys are arguing a lot, I can clear out that storage in the apartment over the garage."

"Nah, we're fine. We both work so much, we're not even here a lot together."

What I don't tell him is that some nights when the house is quiet, all I can think about is what she's doing in her room. Is she masturbating to visuals of me? Will the sexual tension between us ever evaporate?

"Okay, I appreciate it. I was worried about Derek retaliating somehow, but I was thankful to get that call from the police in Washington."

"For sure. I'm already making a success of my charter

boat. Speaking of, let's set up a boys' trip. I'll take all you guys out."

He runs a hand through his hair. The bags under his eyes say raising twins isn't easy. "That would be awesome. We finally have the twins on a good sleep schedule, but when they're awake, it's mayhem."

I laugh. "The sheriff's being run ragged by two little ones?"

"Hell yeah, I am." His phone goes off. "And that would be Allie." He stands.

"Hey, if you need me to babysit for you and Allie so you can go out sometime, just say the word."

His head falls back in laughter. "I hate to break it to you, but you'd need reinforcements."

"Gunner and I can handle it."

He holds out his fist to me. "You and your inflated ego always think you can do anything."

I bump his fist, and he opens the door, stepping outside. We say goodbye, and I shut the door and turn, staring up the stairs. Maybe that's what that moment was in the bathroom—my inflated ego assuming Chevelle wants me the same way I want her.

Chapter Twelve

Chevelle

Cam comes downstairs, tying his tie that matches his suit. Even though it's only been a couple weeks since I saw Cam dressed up now that he wears T-shirts, sweatshirts, and shorts to work, I forgot how sexy he looks in a suit. "Can I ride with you?"

"What's it worth to you?" I ask, finishing my coffee.

He straightens the knot in his tie in the reflection of the small mirror by the back door. Turning around, his eyes take me in. I don't often wear a dress, so I get his surprise. I just wish I could ignore the desire in his gorgeous brown eyes.

We're heading to the adoption ceremony for Adam and Lucy and their new baby girl. I opted for a navy wrap dress that stops a few inches above my knee and paired it with a set of heels that hopefully make my legs look great. Based on Cam's reaction, I picked right.

"You mean what'll I give you in return?" He walks toward me.

My breath halts and he reaches past me, grabbing a coffee mug from behind me on the counter. He smells magnificent. I want him to stay right where he is, but he steps back and smiles at me.

"A charter?" I say with raised eyebrows and a smirk.

"Yeah, right. I'm the low one on the list so far." He pours coffee into a mug and sits at the table.

Thankfully, he *is* last on the list right now. Rowdy is number two and I'm number one. I've been able to keep a level head and not brag too much. I'm afraid if I do, one of them will sabotage one of my charters.

"Does it bother you?" I stay a safe distance away from his gorgeous body that smells too good not to touch.

"Does what?" He leans back in the chair and looks at me.

"Not being the best?"

A slow and easy smile crosses his face. "Am I usually the best?"

I regret my choice of words. "I guess what I mean is, does it bother you that you suck at the fishing excursion thing?"

He chuckles. "There's the girl I know."

"What does that mean?" I frown.

"You never want to compliment me."

"I compliment you plenty."

He sips his coffee and swallows. "It doesn't bother me because I'm just getting started. Plus, I don't see it as my endgame. I have other things that are more important to me."

"Like running the marina?"

He shrugs. "Maybe."

"Do you really want to spend all your time cooped up in an office? Have people not like you?" I sit at the table. We have a few minutes before we have to leave.

"And be rich?"

My head tilts. "Is money that important to you?"

"Well, I've never not had it. It's a nice life, I can't lie."

I don't know if he's purposely being this way or if he

thinks he can't be straight with me. Maybe he's afraid to be vulnerable with me.

"I guess we're different in that way then."

"What do you really wanna ask me, Chevelle?"

I stare across the table, and he raises his eyebrows at me. "I guess I'm wondering if you really want to make a living at the fishing excursion thing. You have the personality and arrogance that fishermen would trust. This is your chance to get out from under your dad's thumb."

"With the boat he bought me? With the profits he's taking? I'm far from being out from under my dad's thumb right now."

"Well, maybe you could make arrangements to buy it from him?"

He shakes his head. "You don't get it. My dad wanted to start this business. I never would've put myself in competition with you."

My heart pitter-patters, and I can't help the smile that forms.

"Would I love a life outside of my dad? Hell yes. But I ruined that chance a long time ago. Everyone in this town sees me as the perpetual bachelor who doesn't work for what he has." He rises from the chair, takes a sip of coffee, and dumps the rest in the sink before rinsing the cup.

"That's not true."

He turns and leans against the counter. "Isn't it?"

I open my mouth but shut it, unsure what to say. "Well, *I* don't think that. I think you can do whatever you want and make it a success."

"Thanks for believing in me." He smiles and lets Gunner in the house through the back door. "I'll be out by the car when you're ready."

I dump out my coffee and grab my purse, petting

Gunner as he sits by the front window. He's used to going almost everywhere with us.

I unlock the car and Cam doesn't take long to sit in the passenger seat, buckling himself in.

"You can drive if you want?"

He shakes his head. "Nah, I like you being my chauffeur."

I start the car and pull out of the driveway toward the courthouse. The silence throughout our drive feels like a third passenger. I should've never started that conversation in the kitchen. Cam's future is none of my business.

THE JUDGE's gavel pounds the wood in front of him, finalizing the adoption of little Althea Greene. Marla ushers Trey to join his parents, and the four of them all smile and hug while she takes pictures.

I sit in the courtroom and watch my brother and his wife, their smiles contagious as the rest of our big family swarms them. They've been through so much, and it warms my heart to see them so happy now.

The judge smashes the gavel down again. "I'm happy for you all, but this isn't a movie. You can do this outside the courtroom." She smiles, and my dad apologizes while ushering all of us out.

Like a reception line at a wedding, we each take turns hugging and congratulating Adam and Lucy and welcoming Thea to the family.

"Can I take this off now?" Trey grabs the hem of his "Big Brother" T-shirt and starts lifting it.

"Not yet." Lucy stops him. She looks at me. "I guess when you're eight, you're too cool for T-shirts like this."

"Yes, he is, Luce," Cam tells it how it is.

I did think when I saw Trey sitting next to Marla that those shirts are for younger kids, but I'm not a mother, so what do I know?

Lucy looks at Trey and how miserable he is, then takes a shirt out of her big bag she carries everywhere and hands it over. I swear she has one of everything in there. "Go change in the bathroom. And since Uncle Cam has his opinions, he can go with you."

Cam grabs the shirt. "He's a boy. We can do it right here. Take it off, Trey." Trey doesn't think twice before tearing off the shirt and Cam puts the other shirt over his head and Trey puts his arms in. "Voilà. Not hard."

I laugh and Lucy's head rears back.

"What?" I ask.

"Did you just laugh at something Cam did?" she asks.

All our family members stop what they're doing and stare at me.

"Um..."

Cam swings his arm around my shoulders. "She's softening up to me. Helps that I make her breakfast every morning."

"I have to admit, I thought for sure one of you would kill the other by now," Nikki says, holding a sleeping Noah to her chest.

"We've managed fine," I say.

"I knew we should've bet on it," Jed says, rocking his new baby, Joshua.

All eyes are on us. I want to hide so no one sees that my usual MO of always starting shit with Cam is lessening because I'm with him so much. I'll be the first to admit maybe I didn't know Cameron Baker as well as I thought I did. After all, he hasn't gone on one date since he's moved into my house. He hasn't been partying. He hasn't been a major pig where I'm concerned. In fact, he's been somewhat thoughtful and funny, and...

I shake my head, shutting down that line of thought. A crush on Cam is one thing. Falling for him is something else entirely.

I glance at Fisher, looking at Cam's hand dangling off my neck, dangerously close to my breast. Sliding out of Cam's hold, I pick up my niece Leighton. She's just about to walk and squirms out of my hold.

"She's independent, don't you know," Presley, her mom, says, running her hand over her very pregnant belly.

"She's ready to move," I say.

"If only she wouldn't just rock the furniture and let go. She's like her father." She smiles at my brother, Cade, who rolls his eyes.

"Let's go back to the house. Marla has a ton of food," my dad announces, and everyone follows him out.

Cam ends up meeting me at my car when he could probably have gone with one of my siblings.

"Still riding with me?" I unlock the doors.

"Nah, I'd only be trading down. I'm sticking with you." He slides into the car, driving me crazy with his lines today.

I climb in, buckle my seat belt, and start the car while feeling his gaze on me.

"Does it ever change your mind?" I ask.

"Change my mind?"

"Well, clearly you aren't the settling down type, but seeing all my brothers and sisters with their spouses and children... does it change things for you? Make you think twice about it?" I follow the line of cars like a funeral procession toward my parents' house.

"Does it change it for you?"

"I asked you first," I say, glancing over to see his full attention on me. I quickly look back at the road.

"I've never been against marriage. Although my parents aren't exactly a great example of it. Sure, they've made it work, but my mom bends to my dad's will at every turn. I wouldn't want a wife like that."

I scoff. "Oh really? You'd want one who challenges you? You enjoy fighting every day?"

"Some of my favorite moments in life have been fighting with you."

My heart just about leaps out of my chest, and I glance at him.

He smiles wide. "In all seriousness, I'd never want a woman to just do what I want all the time. One thing I've always admired about your dad and Marla is how they work together—sometimes she gets her way, sometimes he does. I can't imagine being a stepparent to someone and having to walk that line so carefully."

"What do you mean?" I never really thought about my dad and Marla. I don't remember my dad with my mom, unfortunately, so the only example I have of a long-term marriage is my dad's second marriage.

"Well, Marla's kids still have a dad. Sure, they don't have much of a relationship with him, but he's there. I'm sure it's hard for your dad when he might have an opinion on how something should go, but he talks to Marla on the side or doesn't say anything at all. And Marla." He blows out a breath.

"What about her?"

He touches my knee and I jerk, making my foot come off the gas. Cade slams on his horn behind me. I lift my hand to wave sorry.

"She's competing with a memory. I love your siblings,

but your mom is on a pedestal. As she should be. I can't imagine how hard it is for Marla to toe that line, wanting to be a mother to you but knowing she can't replace the one you lost. Add on..."

The car falls silent because he doesn't want to address the biggest issue—me being responsible for my mother's death.

"Add on what, Cam?" The bite in my tone is there to force him off the topic, but I should know that isn't his style.

"Everyone knows how hard it's been for you, is all I'm saying. It probably makes her want to mother you even more."

I've allowed Marla to mother me, but my shame and guilt have probably always stood between us. I need to get rid of this melancholy mood in the car and fast as we approach my dad and Marla's house.

"I forgot to tell you, I have a date tonight. So in case you're looking for me later and wondering where I am..."

He doesn't say anything, but I see his chest rise and fall. I park in our driveway since my dad's is sure to be packed. As soon as the car comes to a stop, he says nothing and climbs out, walking up the hill to my parents'.

I don't really have a date, which means I have to find some way to kill time for a few hours. I feel bad, but it was necessary. I don't need anyone feeling sorrier for me than I already do.

Cam

I have no idea when Chevelle got home because I arrived home later than she did. Instead of driving myself crazy and watching her leave with her date, I worked on my little side project.

By the time I got home, she was already in her room, the light off, but the glare of the television shone through the small opening at the bottom of her door.

I wish I could get her to open up to me about her mother. Her scars are deep, and therapy helped, but I still hear it in her voice—she blames herself. Jesus, she was five and didn't know the ice wasn't solid. She was only in search of her brothers. Her story's haunted this town for years, but as everyone else has moved on, Chevelle still looks at that moment as though it defines her worth.

And of course, she's already gone this morning, so I head to the marina on foot. Which isn't bad because I stop for coffee at The Grind. I reach the marina entrance and my phone rings, but I let it go to voice mail since I have a lot to do to get my boat ready before my charter arrives. The guy who booked it said there's eight of them and they're avid fishermen who pick a different spot every year. If all goes well, it should put me in at least second place on the list.

I pass Rowdy on the dock, who's returning with his break-of-dawn customers.

"Heard you have a lot of guys this mornin'," he says, helping his customers carry their catch to the store to turn it into filets they can take home.

"Yep, be careful, I'm coming for you." I wink and climb aboard my boat.

I look over at Chevelle, who's packing her cooler with drinks. She's wearing her typical gear except she's in pants since this morning is a tad chilly. I like her better in shorts for sure.

A guy catches my eye while I'm cleaning the front of my boat, where most people uninterested in fishing sit. It's actually the most important spot because if the people the fishermen drag along don't have fun, you might never see them again. Luckily my boat is big enough to accommodate.

"I'm looking for Cameron Baker?" I hear the stranger ask Rowdy.

Rowdy points at me and continues on his way.

"How can I help you?" I ask from the boat.

He stands on the dock and looks toward Chevelle instead of at me. "Um... I'm Kevin Irving. We had an excursion booked this morning for eight."

"You're a little early, but it won't take me long to get the boat going. Earlier's better anyway." I look around. "Where's the rest of you?"

He bites the corner of his lip and throws his hand through his grayish-black hair. "That's the thing... we all drank a little too much last night, so we have to cancel. I tried to call, but you didn't answer. Since we're just at the inn, I drew the short stick and had to come and tell you in person." He glances behind him again at Chevelle.

"Where'd you tie one on last night?" I walk down from the boat to join him on the dock.

"Someone told us about a bar in Lake Starlight, Lucky's? And we met…" He turns again in Chevelle's direction. "Do you know if that woman's name is Chevelle?"

My body tenses. Was this her date? "It is. Why?"

He smiles. "Well, she was with us, and we were doing shots. At some point she disappeared, but we had to grab Ubers to bring us back to the inn."

"Oh really?" Date my ass. Anger heats the blood in my veins.

"Yeah. Anyway, I'm sorry to waste your time. I'm sure you're all booked for the day. Chevelle mentioned she had an opening for later this evening, so maybe we'll book with her if we can get our shit together."

He's right, I am booked, but with my dad's people. They might throw their rod in the water, but unless some miracle happens, they'll let it sit there all day while they eat and drink and talk bullshit with each other. None of them are true fishermen.

"When are you in town again? Believe me, you want on this boat. It has more room and I have radar."

He smiles. "Today is our last chance to get a fishing charter in. The wives decided to meet us so…" He shrugs.

"Okay. Well, as you probably know, I have to keep your deposit."

"Yeah, definitely. It was our fault and I'm really sorry about it." He steps back.

"Good luck." I climb back on my boat and stew in my wheelhouse as I watch the guy go over to her.

She smiles at him and nods a bunch, her eyes never venturing over here. This move definitely deserves payback. The fish from this trip would've made my entire week.

Kevin leaves the marina with one last wave. Of course, I'm cordial and friendly because I need him to come back.

Ten minutes later, Chevelle leaves on her charter.

Rowdy calls up to me from the dock. "Can I come aboard?"

"Sure, Rowdy."

He steps on and looks at all the high-end tech equipment in the wheelhouse. He's old school and probably thinks it's all a waste of time.

"Man, how are you in last place when you have all this stuff?" He sits in one of the chairs. "Ah, because your clients are taking naps in these comfy seats."

I chuckle.

"You see those wooden boats with the purple stripe around yet?"

"Just the other day. A lot of people asking about them," I say.

"They're sharp lookin'."

"They are."

"I thought there was only one, but I just saw a second one that's a little different but has the same purple stripe. Sure enough, the same manufacturer name on the side. Five Seas." Rowdy stares at the bay. "No one knows where they're comin' from."

I shrug. "There are new boat makers all the time."

"True. Anyway, that's not why I came on here. You two are playin' dirty."

I hold up my hands. "I'm not."

He raises his eyebrows. "You tell every man who wants to climb on Chevelle's boat that you're her boyfriend. I'm not saying anythin', and I know it ain't right, but some of those men book charters with Chevelle because, well..."

I nod so he doesn't have to say it. I don't really want to hear him say it anyway because it'll just piss me off.

"But if she got your charter drunk last night, then I'd say you could definitely pay her back."

I don't say anything. It's not that I haven't considered it.

"This flirtatious thing goin' on between you two reminds me of me and my dear Anna. She's the same as Chevelle. All tough and don't need no one."

I tip back my coffee. "But I'm not sure that's the truth."

Rowdy shakes his head. "It's not. That girl's out to prove somethin'. Like she wants everyone in this town to stop feeling sorry for her. And I wish she'd just accept the fact that she lost her mama and whether you're five or sixty-five, losing your mama is not somethin' people get over."

"She blames herself."

He nods. "Don't know anyone who wouldn't."

"And that's the problem."

"You can't solve this for her." Rowdy eyes me as if I don't understand.

"I can't take away her pain, but I can hold her hand through it."

Rowdy smiles, his gold tooth in the back gleaming. "Good luck. That shell is thick and strong from years of keepin' her pain hidden." He pats me on the back. "I have to get ready for my next one, and don't worry, the fish costume ain't that bad."

He steps off my boat and walks over to his more modest fishing boat. I'm not even sure he offers snacks. But the man knows his clientele well. They'd probably just chuck snacks overboard.

I pull my phone out of my pocket and type out all the supplies I need to give Chevelle the payback she deserves after ruining my best charter of the month.

LATER THAT NIGHT, I'm sitting at the kitchen table in the dark, trying unsuccessfully to work on my laptop. Anything to distract me from my feelings for Chevelle. It was so much easier when we didn't live together. When I didn't have to witness the small moments in her life. When I didn't know what she looks like when she gets up in the morning, or what TV shows she likes to unwind with at the end of a long day, or how she takes her coffee.

"Damn it!" I hear, then *bang, bang, bang* and a plate crashing and breaking on the floor. "Shit."

I jump out of the chair and rush out of the room, flicking on the light in the foyer.

"Turn it off!" Chevelle yells, so I quickly turn the light back off. "I'm naked."

You have to be fucking kidding me.

"Do you have someone over? I thought we said no guests." My hands fist at my sides.

"No." She huffs. "I sleep naked."

"Oh hell, why'd you just tell me that?" I whine. Now I'll be imagining her in bed every night not wearing a stitch of clothes.

"A lot of people sleep naked."

"I know that, it's just..." I huff. "What happened? Are you okay?"

"I woke up and couldn't get back to sleep, so I was just bringing a plate down. I didn't think you were still awake! I slipped on the stairs, and when I went to catch myself, the plate fell and broke. I don't want to step on any of the pieces. Can you get me a shirt and shorts to put on?"

"In order to do that, I have to go up the stairs."

"Shit," she says.

"I'll cover my eyes. Let me just turn on the light."

"No! You'll see me naked."

"Well, the only piece of clothing I have on is my track shorts."

"Perfect, give them to me."

I roll my eyes. "Then I'll be naked."

She's silent for a moment. "Well, be the gentleman anyway."

I laugh. "I've seen naked women before."

"And I've seen naked guys."

"In fact, I saw you naked for a split second in Hawaii... remember?" My blood heats from thinking about that flash of bare skin I saw when we had to share a room and ran into each other when she was coming out of the shower wearing just a towel.

"Well then, it's time for me to see you naked. Give me the shorts."

Huh. She's got me there. "But..."

"Let me guess, I've never seen one as big as yours?"

I chuckle. "Probably not, not that I wanted to brag."

Another bout of silence falls over the foyer.

"I could toss you my phone," I say. "You could use my flashlight to see."

"Oh, good idea. Do that."

I go back into the kitchen and turn on the light.

"Cam!"

"I'm not facing you. I have to see where my phone is."

"Right. Okay, sorry."

I spot my phone on the table, grab it, and turn off the kitchen light. "Okay, I'll toss it to you."

"Okay, I'm right here." I toss in the direction of her voice and all I hear is the phone bang on the floor wherever it landed. "Didn't you play football?"

"I was the receiver, not the quarterback. If you're gonna judge so much, maybe I'll just leave you there."

"This is so frustrating."

"You're a woman and I'm a man. We can see each other naked. It's not the end of the world."

"Speak for yourself."

I let my chin drop to my chest. "Even if I give you my shorts, it'll only cover your lower half."

She doesn't say anything.

"Okay. Okay. I'll turn on the light in the foyer and go back to the kitchen. You can see where all the broken pieces are and maybe you can get back upstairs and be fine."

"Good idea. Why didn't we already think of that?"

Because all the blood is rushing to my cock.

"Okay, I'm turning it on in three, two, one." I turn on the light and leave the foyer.

"Shit, I fell right in the middle of the broken plate and I'm bleeding."

"Game over, Chevelle." I walk out of the kitchen, seeing her naked on the stairs with little pieces of yellow plate around her.

"Cam!" She whips one arm over her breasts and the other between her legs to cover her mound.

"I'm done with the games. I'm not gonna let you sit there bleeding. You're hot as fuck and have nothing to be insecure about with me seeing you naked. If it makes you feel better." I push off my shorts, leaving me standing naked across from her. "Now we're both naked."

She laughs and I instinctively want to cover my junk. "This is insane."

"You don't laugh in the presence of a man's dick, Chevelle."

"It's not that, it's just... I can't believe this. All the times I've... and now."

"All the times what?" I kneel and grab the larger pieces of the plate.

"Nothing."

I stand to throw away what I have and grab the broom and dustpan from the kitchen. "Chevelle Greene, have you wondered what I look like naked?"

Her cheeks turn red. "Just clean up the mess so I can get dressed."

I look up at her and our eyes lock. The space between us feels like an elastic band that's been stretched too wide. The tension is palpable and about to break. My cock hardens past the full chub it was and Chevelle takes notice.

Jesus, I'd do just about anything to take her right where she is. Without the shards of a broken plate surrounding her, obviously. Though if that image isn't a visual representation of what it would mean for me to be with my best friend's little sister, I don't know what is.

"I've thought about you naked a lot too, if it matters."

We lock eyes but she doesn't say anything, so I get to work.

"I can honestly say this is a first for me." I sweep up the mess so she can stand. "Get up and go to the couch. I'll finish cleaning."

She does as I ask, and I check out her ass over my shoulder. Just as perfect as I knew it would be.

"You tell no one about this," she warns.

"My lips are sealed."

After I clean up the broken plate with the broom and a wet paper towel, I pull on my shorts.

"I have one question. If you didn't trip, would you have walked into the kitchen naked?" I ask.

She's wrapped herself in a blanket that was across the back of the sofa. "I didn't know you were down here. What were you doing anyway?"

"Just working on something." I want to tell her what no one knows, but I'm not ready. "It should be good for you to go back up now."

She nods and stands, leaving the room. "Cam?"

I turn to find her standing at the bottom of the stairs.

"Thank you."

"Sweet dreams, Chevelle." She slowly climbs the stairs, and once I can't see her anymore, I glance at my dick. "I know, buddy, I wish that went differently too."

Chapter Fourteen

Chevelle

*O*ut of all my sisters, Posey is the closest to my age, so I text her on my way to work because I really need to talk to someone about this sexual tension with Cam. The fact he saw me naked three days ago but acts as if he didn't conflict with the part of me that was convinced that, at the very least, he was attracted to me.

After work, I plan to head to Posey's house for help down this blind path I'm on. With all the guys I've ever liked, it was easy. I like them and am attracted to them, so I date them, and if we like one another, we have sex when we both feel comfortable. It lasts for a while and it's fun, and when it's not fun anymore, we part ways. But none of the guys I've been into is my brother's best friend.

I park my car in the marina lot. My first excursion today is with four older ladies who are very straitlaced, so I'm almost completely covered up this morning. Last time they made comments about how too much of my skin was show-ing. Need I remind them it was, like, eighty degrees and I'd been outside the entire day? But I don't want to offend, and thankfully it's cooler today.

"Mornin', Chevelle," Vinny says, grinning.

"Someone looks happy to be back home."

From the looks of it, Vinny's boat just returned, since

most of his fishermen are filing out toward the wholesale distributor where their catch will be weighed and paid out.

I walk down the plank and glance in Cam's direction. Things haven't been awkward between us. In fact, Cam has acted completely normal since we saw one another naked.

"Morning," Cam says, raising his coffee mug.

"Chevelle," Rowdy says with a nod.

Man, everyone is super friendly this morning.

I'm halfway to my boat when Heidi, one woman in the group I'm taking out, calls from behind me, "Oh good, you're here. We were browsing the gift shop until you showed up. Thank goodness it was open."

Heidi is decked out in camo gear as if we need to hide from the fish to catch them, but I don't ask why.

"You're here early. I wasn't expecting you for another half hour." Which left me time to make sure the boat seats were wiped down and to stock the coolers. Although these women don't drink, I like to have some beer on hand just in case.

"Well, they're all excited." She turns toward the store, where the other three women are huddled together. "LADIES!"

I open my jaw and press a finger to my ear in an attempt to relieve the pain in my ears.

The three other women meet us where we're standing.

"Ladies, just give me five minutes to wipe down the seats and make sure I have enough refreshments."

They all hold up their jugs.

"No need. We brought our own," Heidi says.

"We don't believe in plastic bottles," Cindy says.

"Horrible for the environment," says the third, who I always think of as bird lady because she always wears clothing with birds on it.

"Are you going to have kids one day? If so, you want to leave them a healthy planet." Stella, the fourth woman, touches my arm.

"Okay then, no water, but still give me five minutes to wipe down the boat from overnight." I turn and walk toward my boat.

"We'll help. We're a bunch of eager beavers this morning," Heidi says.

"Women helping women is what it's all about." Stella comes up beside me. "Seriously though, think about the bottled water thing."

I nod and smile, which is my normal response with this charter.

When we board my boat, Heidi gasps and each woman takes her turn gasping before I really make sense of what I'm looking at. My boat is covered in cheap lingerie, condom wrappers, condoms, vibrators, dildos, and an open bottle of lube, a long line squeezed out on the bench. In addition to all the sex crap, there are empty alcohol bottles and red Solo cups.

I swivel around and everybody who works on the dock is laughing. Cam raises his coffee mug at me. That son of a bitch.

"Um... Chevelle." Heidi swallows a bunch of times. "Is your boat used for other things besides fishing?"

"No. Someone must've done this without my knowing."

Anger fires up inside me. I'm going to kill him.

"Well, I'm sorry, I cannot clean that up and I cannot get on that boat." Stella shakes her head.

"Filthy sex things happened here last night," Cindy whispers to me.

"No, it's a prank."

"A prank?" bird lady asks.

"Yes, there's a competition going on. Please, ladies, give me a minute to clean this up, and we'll be on our way."

They shake their heads, all four of them retreating down the pier.

"We'll reschedule, honey, you just... do you." Then they all turn and speed walk out of the marina.

I scream and it echoes through the still morning air. "Cameron Baker!"

I stomp down my dock to his. Everyone steps out of my way, smiling and laughing.

He looks over the edge of his boat. "Can I help you?"

"Did you do that?" I stab my finger in the direction of my boat.

"Well." He shrugs. "If memory serves, you got my biggest charter drunk the night before and told them you had an opening. So... yeah, I did. Did Heidi and the girls not like it? Sorry, I thought you'd be here early enough to clean it up."

"You did not. You did it on purpose so I'd lose a charter and have to wear the damn fish costume." I climb on board and poke him in the chest. "Mine was by accident."

He stares down at my finger, and I clench my fist, moving it to my side. "It was not an accident. You knew they were my charter."

"Not right away, I didn't."

"But?"

She says nothing.

"Fess up, Chevelle."

She sighs and juts out her hip. "The one guy started talking about the boat he'd booked and how awesome it was. It was easy to figure out they were talking about yours."

"And you sabotaged me."

Ugh. I hate when he's right. "Maybe. But they were

ordering the majority of the shots, okay?" I shake my head and let out a sound of frustration.

"Now we're even."

I laugh in his face. "We're not even. You better watch around every corner, Cameron Baker, because when I'm out for revenge, I go for the throat."

I stomp off his boat and down the pier. "I'm sure all these items came from your personal collection, so you better come get them before I throw them all out."

"It was a joke, Chevelle. You took away one of mine and I took away one of yours."

I give him the finger while walking away. "Of course, Cam. No hard feelings."

I ENDED up canceling on Posey because there's no more sexual tension between Cam and me. Not after what he did.

I've waited four days to pull this prank because it's been fun watching his paranoia in action. Sitting down but standing up quickly, thinking I left a tack on his seat. He peeks through every door before entering the room, and he's always looking over his shoulder.

In truth, I probably don't even have to do anything because the threat alone is doing the trick. But I have to hit him where it hurts, which is his charters. He has to feel my wrath there for it to be payback.

He walks down the stairs in the morning like usual, peeking around the corner before walking into the kitchen.

"Calm down, Cam."

"What did you do?" he asks.

I was going to make him breakfast and coffee, but I thought he'd never eat or drink anything from me, so I didn't bother. "I figured we'd walk into work together, stop at The Grind, get some coffee and a muffin."

His eyes narrow the slightest bit. "What's your game plan? String me up in the town square and leave paddles for kids to hit me?"

I laugh because the image is funny. "You need to relax. Maybe I'm not going to do anything. I just figured the weather is cooling down and pretty soon we won't be able to walk to work."

He nods slowly. "Okay."

"Good. Let me grab my bag and we'll leave."

He lets Gunner out back and eyes me the entire time I'm getting everything together as though I'm going to pull out a paintball gun and shoot him in the nuts or something.

Gunner comes back in the house and we both leave, me locking the door. The entire time we walk, he's on the side away from the road.

"I'm not going to push you in front of a car, Cam."

"Maybe not, but I'm more comfortable on this side."

"If you're so worried about retaliation, why'd you do it in the first place?"

He chuckles. "Because it was payback for what you did."

"Yeah, so maybe I'm not gonna do anything."

"I'd feel more comfortable if you just said you weren't."

"But what fun would that be?" I waggle my eyebrows.

He shakes his head, and we cross the street to The Grind.

I've learned a lot about Cam since we've been living together. One is that he is a man of routine. He buys his coffee, sets it on the boat, and wipes the benches and seats free from the morning dew while his coffee cools a bit. So all I need to do is to get him on his boat and I can slip him the laxative.

We order our coffees, and he is a stickler, always wanting to pay, so I let him.

On the way to the marina, I make casual conversation. "Is your dad easing up at all? You've had some successful charters lately. Maybe not ones that brought in a lot of fish, but ones where people were having fun. You're a born entertainer."

"Are you buttering me up for something?" He narrows his eyes as though he's trying to figure out my game.

I laugh. "No, I'm just asking."

He shrugs. "Nothing yet. He's still acting like I'm doing this on my own, but he sends me customers. This is just another way for him to keep me under his thumb."

"But he wanted you out from under his thumb."

He shakes his head. "That's not what he really wants. He just wants to control me. Have me do this his way."

"Then why cut you off?"

We enter the marina, and it's quiet this morning, which is my favorite kind of morning here. When the fishermen are gone, Rowdy is gone. Usually when the tourist season winds down is when we get this peace and quiet first thing in the morning.

"He cut me off because I embarrassed him by beating up Derek," Cam says.

"But—"

"Regardless of the reason. I didn't act like the owner of a marina should. I should've kept my feelings out of it. Plus, he wanted to start this whole charter thing anyway. I told him no two months ago, so this allowed him the opportunity to force me to do it. He wanted to kick Rowdy out because he was... never mind, I shouldn't be telling you this."

"You can trust me." I might put a laxative in his drink,

but that's just our competition. I'd never betray his trust on a personal level.

"Rowdy was behind on his rent, so I paid his fees on my own credit card. My dad probably figured it out somehow, and the fight was just his way of getting me in line again."

He walks toward his boat, and I follow.

"I'm sorry, Cam."

He shrugs. "I have my own plans. They're in the works. Just not ready to be revealed yet."

"What are they?" I follow.

He doesn't object to me being on his boat, putting his coffee on the ledge in his wheelhouse as I predicted. He picks up a towel and wipes down the seats and benches. "I'm not ready to talk about it just yet."

"Okaaay." Although I'm dying to know, I act indifferent.

"I gotta grab a new rag. I'll be right back."

He goes to the galley of the boat, and I go over to pour the liquid laxative into his coffee. Just a splash so he can't successfully navigate today's charters. I don't want him getting really sick.

Maybe I should let this go. Say we're even after the two instances. But I just know I've lost Heidi and her gang forever, and even if I don't particularly like the people, money is money. And everyone thought the prank was so funny.

"Sorry, Cam." I pour in a small amount of liquid. I don't want him shitting his pants or anything.

He comes back up with two rags.

"I better go. I have an early charter too. Thanks for the coffee and muffin." I raise my cup.

He smiles. "It was a nice walk."

"It was. Catch you later."

"Good luck today," he says.

"You too." I barely keep the grin off my face.

I walk down the pier and over to my boat. I watch Cam the whole time, thankful when I see him take a break and sip his coffee.

Smiling to myself, I wait for the fun to begin. At least for me.

Chapter Fifteen

Chevelle

I keep looking at Cam's boat, and he's yet to run to the bathroom, from what I can tell. He's been casually sitting in his wheelhouse on his phone with his feet propped up, drinking his coffee. The coffee I put the laxative in.

I open my bag and yes, it was the right bottle.

Having no choice but to leave when my charter arrives, he waves at me as we're leaving. "Safe trip." His smile is so wide, it tells me I'm missing something.

I wave back.

"Is that Cameron Baker?" the dad on the charter asks.

"It is." Most of our charter guests come from out of town, but this family said they just wanted a day away and made the impromptu decision two days ago to book my charter. Thankfully, I was available. "How do you know him?"

"He and his friend come to me all the time. He's watching his friend more often than not."

The mom lowers her book. "My husband's a tattoo artist. Owns Smokin' Guns in Lake Starlight."

I nod. "Oh yeah. I think I've heard of it."

"Does he have a younger brother?" The teenage daughter is practically hanging out of the boat, looking back at the pier.

I laugh. "Sorry, only child."

The mom looks up from her book again. "And that man is way too old for you, sweetie."

"Is he your boyfriend?" the girl asks.

"Cam? No. He's my brother's best friend. I grew up with him."

"Oh!" The girl looks at her mom, who's smiling at her husband. "My dad was my mom's brother's best friend."

"Really?" I smile.

"I still am their best friend," the dad says.

The mom leans over. "It took me a long time to admit my feelings."

The big guy with more tattoos than Fisher moves to sit next to his wife, setting his hand on her knee. "But I wore her down."

"Now they're gonna kiss," their son whines and covers his eyes.

After their chaste kiss, we're out of the marina and on our way to a fishing location that I hope will be successful for the little boy because it would suck if he didn't catch anything. Once we're there, the mom sits with me while the dad puts bait on the kids' hooks.

"So there's nothing between you two?" She actually catches me off guard and the look I give her causes her to step back, hand raised. "Sorry, I sound like my grandma."

I can't help but chuckle. "My grandma too. In fact, if I didn't know better, I'd suspect she booked your charter to get the skinny on Cam and me."

She laughs and looks at me for a moment. "I think I know you, actually. Do you have a brother who plays soccer?"

"I do."

She points at herself. "Savannah Bailey—er, Kelly. But my niece Calista plays with your brother... Rylan, right?"

My eyes widen. "You're a Bailey?"

"Was a Bailey!" her husband calls from the front of the boat.

"Liam, I'll always be a Bailey," she says.

"Nope, you're a Kelly." He looks at his children. "We're Kellys."

Savannah laughs. I thought she looked familiar, but I see so many people during tourist season it's hard to keep them all straight.

"So your grandma is Dori Bailey?"

"The one and only," Savannah says. "And I swear she did not send me here." She holds up both hands this time.

We laugh, and just then, Cam's boat goes by, venturing farther out. He's at the helm, the wind blowing his hair, his charter guests all laughing, and a woman at his side is chatting him up. She's attractive and definitely his type.

Why the hell isn't he in the bathroom by now?

I watch them pass, and he doesn't even give me a wave or a hello.

I look at Savannah, who's giving me a knowing smile. "Your secret is safe with me." She looks at her husband and kids. "God knows, it took me forever to get where we are."

"It's not..." But I stop, because why lie to this woman? "It's just complicated."

She puts her hand on mine. "Oh, I know. Believe me, I know."

FOR THE REST of the day, Cam and I pass one another on the water. He doesn't look uncomfortable. He's not sweating. He even stopped and talked to Liam Kelly for a good half hour and was his usual charming self. He's taken out all of his charters, helped them carry the fish in, and nothing. What am I missing?

It isn't until the end of the day, when we're both cleaning out our boats, that he calls my name. Rowdy has already left the marina, and the majority of the fishing boats are gone for the week.

"Chevelle!" he says. "Come over and have a beer."

"No, thanks."

"Oh, come on. It's been a long day for both of us."

And he's right. It has. So I leave my boat, since it's already clean, and walk over to his. Since he's in one of the more expensive slips, he's pretty much all by himself. The yachts we get here in the nice weather are dwindling as we come to the end of the season.

I slip off my shoes and step on his boat. He offers me a beer, and I accept it.

"If you prefer, I have some coffee from this morning." He jiggles an empty cup in the air.

I frown and shake my head.

"Did you really think I'd drink something that was left in your presence without me?"

"It was worth a try after what you did to me."

He goes down to the galley, and I follow. "I admit the orgy thing wasn't nice. But I did think you were going to get there before them. And let's remember, you're responsible for the dead fish and for getting my customers drunk the night before."

"I told you I had no idea they were your customers until it was too late."

He turns around and steps toward me, pushing my body against the counter. "And the laxative in the coffee?"

"What do you care? You didn't even drink it."

"No, but one of my guests did. I left it on the wheelhouse counter, and she mistook it for her own. Was in the bathroom the entire charter."

"You mean the blonde?"

He smirks. That arrogant smirk that gets under my skin. I shouldn't have said I even noticed the blonde.

"Was someone following me?" he singsongs.

"You passed me on the boat. She was hard to miss."

He leans in closer, and even after a day's work, I still smell a hint of his cologne. "Are you jealous, Chevelle?"

"Not now that I know she spent the majority of the time in the bathroom." I give him a saccharine smile.

His gaze falls to my lips, and my tongue instinctively slides out of my mouth, licking my bottom lip.

"Admit it." His voice is husky.

"Admit what? That the laxative was for you?"

His hand presses against the ceiling, and he leans in. I lean back as far as I can go, and he shakes his head.

"Get over yourself, Cam."

He shakes his head again. "I'm not buying it. That woman got you jealous, just like all those guys you charter get me riled up."

Our eyes lock.

"I don't want you to win the contest." It's the truth. Even if I'm avoiding a more obvious truth.

"And I don't want you to win, but right now, we're not talking about fish. I want a truce."

I arch my back. The ache building between my legs from feeling his body so close to mine keeps intensifying. He notices and glances down at my pushed-out breasts.

"Fine, you have a truce," I say.

"As easy as that? I don't believe you."

"Ugh." I slide out from under his arm, crossing the room to get some distance. "You're impossible." I start to go up the stairs, but he grabs my wrist.

I stop, and his thumb runs along the inside of my wrist, making my eyes flutter closed for a beat. Then I turn toward him, and he tugs me into his arms.

"Just so you know, I hate you."

"Keep telling yourself that," he whispers right before his lips touch mine.

I try to remain strong, but finally having his lips on mine, after all this time, is my undoing. His tongue slides along my bottom lip, asking permission, and I open for him immediately. We've gone from zero to sixty in three seconds. Neither of us can get enough. My hands fist his shirt, afraid this moment might end. A moment I've waited so damn long for.

His hands venture down my body, grabbing my ass, lifting me so I wrap my legs around his waist. He turns us around and sets me on the edge of the table.

"You know you don't hate me." His lips trail small kisses along my jaw and down my neck.

"Stop talking and keep kissing me."

That cocky smirk is sexy as hell as I fist his shirt and pull him into me. Our movements are frantic and wild. The hunger between us is alive and building, impossible to stop.

My fingers fly to his shorts, unbuttoning and unzipping them, pushing them down. Cam tears off my shirt, leaving me wearing only my bra. His hands mold to my breasts, and he squeezes them, then his thumbs dip below the cups to tease my nipples. All our movements are frantic and jerky, as though if we don't do this right now, we're worried the other one might put a stop to it.

My head falls back on a sigh. "Don't stop."

He unhooks my bra, helping me toss it somewhere to the side.

"You have no idea how much I've wanted to do this." He bends and takes my right nipple into his mouth while his fingers play with my other one.

I put my hands on the table behind me, arching my back for him.

He takes off his shirt, pulling it by the collar over his head, and stares at me for a second. There's something different in his expression than just lust. "Are you sure?"

"Am I sure? Cam, I'm half naked and begging here. I'm sure."

"Okay."

After that, we accomplish getting my shorts and panties off and removing his boxer briefs. I lie on the table, and he grabs my ass, pulling me to the edge while he reaches into a nearby drawer and grabs a condom. I watch him roll it down his considerable length.

"There's so much more I want to do." I run my hand down his chiseled abs. This man has the body of a professional athlete.

"We have time, but right now, I need inside of you." He teases me with the tip of his dick, running it over my clit and making sure I'm wet enough to take him. "You're so fucking beautiful, Chevelle."

He hammers inside me, and I cry out, the feeling of being so full of him intense. "Don't say nice things unless you mean them."

He laughs but doesn't stop drilling me while one hand explores my body, traveling through the valley of my breasts and down my stomach until he reaches my clit. He puts light pressure on the small bud and that orgasm that's been there, waiting on the cusp, flickers to life.

I'm a begging, panting mess beneath him, and he watches me with an intense stare filled with lust and hunger. For some reason, it brings me to the brink when our eyes lock. My hips fly off the table and he slows the rhythm slightly as my vision goes black and ecstasy fills my veins.

Once he knows I've come, he removes his hand from my clit, grabs my hips, and hammers in and out of me before his back arches and he stills inside me, coming on a groan.

I lie sweaty and exhausted below him as he slowly withdraws out of me, leaning forward and kissing the valley between my breasts. "Stay here. I'll be right back."

I try to gather my thoughts as I lie there waiting for him to return. That was intense. Like a firecracker that flared hot and fast before crashing back toward earth.

He disappears into the bathroom. I smile because that was some orgasm. The best ever. I've never been that desperate and frantic to be with a man in all my life.

A phone vibrates somewhere, and I sit up to make sure it's not mine. I grab Cam's phone off the couch beside the table and see Fisher's name on the screen. Then I hear another phone buzzing, which must be mine. I drop Cam's and search for mine.

I'm bent over when Cam returns, his hands grabbing my ass. "I like this view."

Finding my phone, I see the text message that Presley is having the baby.

I turn to Cam, and suddenly everything is so awkward now that my family is front and center.

"Oh god." I grab my clothes. "That can never happen again."

"Why?" He frowns and steps forward.

"I have to get to the hospital." I hurriedly dress and rush off the boat.

What have I done? I slept with him, and now things can never go back to normal. Especially now that I know how good we are together.

Chapter Sixteen

Cam

I catch up to Chevelle in the marina parking lot. "Hold up."

She stops at her car. "Didn't you see your phone? Presley's in labor."

I sigh and stare at her. She cannot ignore what just happened between us. Or maybe she can. She's doing a pretty damn good job of it right now.

I climb into her passenger seat since I still don't have a vehicle. I need to get a car at some point, but it hasn't been a priority since I live so close to the docks. The odd time I've had to travel out of town, I've just taken an Uber.

She backs up and drives way too fast toward the hospital.

"Last I checked, you're not the one having the baby." I grip her door handle before I fall into her when she makes a left turn.

I know what she's doing. She's driving fast because the sooner she gets us there, the sooner we'll be swallowed up by her family. And then what just happened can be forgotten—at least for a while.

"Can we please talk?" I ask.

She has no choice but to stop at a red light, and our bodies fall forward until our seat belts tighten and we're thrown back into our seats. "There's nothing to talk about. It was just a release of sexual tension. I mean, we saw each other naked a few days ago. It was bound to happen."

"But—"

The light turns green, and she slams on the gas. "You don't owe me anything, Cam. It's fine. You're acting like you took my virginity."

I lean back in the passenger seat. Fuck, is she right? Am I acting clingy?

No. This thing between us has been brewing for a long time, and I know her mind was as blown as mine by how good we are together.

"You're right. Sexual tension spurred it, but it doesn't change the fact that I want to see where this goes. I'll talk to your brothers."

She looks at me as though I'm a lunatic. "Um... you are not talking to my brothers."

She pulls into the hospital parking lot, parking next to all the other Greene family cars.

"Yeah, I am. They should know my intentions."

"Your intentions?"

I reach for her hand. "To date you. Get to know you better."

"You've known me since I was five," she says, taking the keys and exiting the car.

I follow suit and jog to catch up to her. "You know what I mean. Are you really denying this?"

"Are you really suggesting this?" There's a softness in her expression for a moment, but the doors to the hospital open and we overhear Ethel arguing with a nurse, so that softness disappears. "It was just sex, Cam."

She walks away to join her grandma at the counter.

"Still hitching rides with my little sister?" Fisher comes up to me holding a squirmy Laurie.

"Hey, man, we need to talk."

His forehead wrinkles. "What about?"

"Well... eh..."

"How nice of Cade and Presley to include us," Ethel says, glancing at Jed and interrupting the conversation I want to have with Fisher.

But as eager as I am to get his blessing, this probably isn't the time.

Jed throws his hands in the air. "For the love of..."

Molly rocks their baby boy, Joshua, shaking her head at the continued guilt trip the family is still laying on her and Jed after they didn't tell anyone when she was in labor a few months ago.

"You made me miss seeing one of my great-grandchildren being born," Ethel says.

"I told you, he came fast. We didn't have any time," Jed continues to argue.

I'm fairly sure he's lying. He and Molly probably just wanted it to be the two of them. Emelia was already at Cade and Presley's for the night since Jed and Molly were doing a date night. Hell, they probably had sex to induce labor.

"There's always next time," Posey says.

"And I called you as soon as it was over," Jed says.

Marla sits in the corner, rocking Shay, Posey and Gavin's new little girl. She doesn't look bothered that Jed didn't call them. Except for Chevelle, every one of the Greene clan is married, and the majority have kids now. Xavier and Clara are in San Francisco since it's football season, and Mandi and Noah are out on one of his photo shoots, so the waiting room isn't as crowded as it normally would be when one of them is having a baby.

Chevelle sits on the floor next to Axel and plays with the toys the hospital has for children. Soon, Noah, Nikki's son, joins, and Leighton, Cade's daughter, whines to get out of Hank's lap. She's wearing her "Big Sister" shirt. Before she realizes it, Chevelle is surrounded by her nieces and nephews, all vying for her attention.

I sit in a chair and watch her interact with them. How natural it is for her to take a book out of Axel's mouth or put the rings in the right order with Leighton. She's going to be a great mother.

Chevelle looks at me, and I smile, but she turns away. She's really struggling with the fact that we slept together. I'm not gonna lie, it was the best sex of my life. I don't know if it's because it's Chevelle and I've waited years to have her, but I want her again and again and again. I don't know that I could ever get enough of her.

For the next couple hours, people pace, get coffee, go for walks.

Allie has to start her shift, so when Fisher becomes responsible for both twins, he says, "We're out. I have to work in the morning, and if I don't get these two asleep, they'll be nightmares tomorrow."

I stand to walk Fisher out, and Chevelle narrows her eyes at me.

"Well, I'm sitting right here. I'm not going to miss another birth," Ethel says.

Jed rolls his eyes with Emelia asleep on his lap. Molly holds Joshua and gives Jed a knowing look. He rises from his seat, Emelia draped in his arms. "We're out too."

One by one, the siblings leave with their babies, leaving me, Chevelle, Ethel and gang, Hank and Marla.

"You can go," Chevelle says.

"I'm good."

"But you don't have to be here."

I shrug. "Cade is my friend."

"Fisher's your friend."

I stare at her for a long time and catch Dori and Midge watching us. I put on a smile to not alert them of anything. "Fine." I stand. "Let me know how it goes. I've got an early charter tomorrow." I stretch. Chevelle doesn't want me here, so I'm not going to stay where I'm not wanted.

"Hopefully we'll have some news soon." Marla rocks Leighton. "You go too, Chevelle. We'll keep you all posted."

I look at the clock and see that it's one in the morning.

"She could be in labor all night," Hank says.

"I thought your second just fell out?" Chevelle says.

He laughs and looks at Marla. "Laurie ended up having a C-section with Chevelle after the boys flew out."

"You just never know." Marla smiles at Chevelle, but Chevelle doesn't return it.

"Okay, call us when the little one arrives." Chevelle kisses all the cheeks of her loved ones around the room.

"Oh, I should tell you two now. I booked you for next week's health and fitness segment." Ethel points at us.

"What?" Chevelle looks irritated.

"The retirement home thinks it's important for us to learn how to eat better and do some yoga and light weights and things." Dori rolls her eyes. "I guess we can't even enjoy our older years without people making us feel guilty."

"And I signed you two up for the fitness portion. Teach us how to use the weights. Chevelle's always been so flexible. You must be good at yoga." Ethel smiles.

"We're not personal trainers," Chevelle says.

"No, dear, but you both spend a lot of time at the gym. We just need the basics," Ethel says.

"Okay, send me the time. No dirty talk though. I've heard

rumors." I eye Midge, who's a kleptomaniac and sex addict from what I can gather.

She pushes her black glasses up on her nose. "Talk to the men in the group."

We leave the hospital, and thankfully Chevelle doesn't say anything about giving me a ride home.

Halfway to the house, I turn in my seat. "Why are you being so dismissive about us?"

For a moment, I don't think she's going to say anything. I take a sip of the water I bought at the hospital.

"I'm not being dismissive. We had sex to ease some sexual frustration and I'm fine with it, but it doesn't mean anything. I'm not looking for a ring or anything."

I choke on my water, and she raises her eyebrows at me.

"Something scary?" she asks.

"No."

She pulls into the driveway and gets out of her car. I follow and shut and lock the front door behind us.

"So your mind is made up, huh?" I ask as she's about to head upstairs.

She turns and throws her hands in the air. "What are you thinking? That you'll do candlelight dinners for me, and we'll make out in the square? That people won't be placing bets on how long we'll last?"

Her comment throws me, and I look at her, trying to figure out what gossip has to do with us.

"Come on, Cam. We're one and the same. Both afraid of commitment, never allowing anyone to get too close, and we have meaningless sex all the damn time. I made peace with myself a long time ago." She turns back around and walks up the stairs. I hear her bedroom door faintly click shut.

I head to the kitchen and grab a beer, let Gunner out, and sit on the back porch with him. The air is much cooler at night than it was even a few weeks ago. Fall is approaching fast. Gunner does his business and sits next to me, so I pet him.

Chevelle's not wrong. I am afraid of commitment, but for some reason, after we had sex, that immediate fear that usually sets in as I wonder whether the girl is going to think it means something it doesn't, wasn't present. I'm ready to go all in on dating Chevelle because something with us just feels right.

But in order to do that, there are a few steps I have to take first. One, talk to her brothers. Two, let her in. Maybe if I do that, she'll let me in too.

I finish my beer and grab a water on my way to my bedroom.

After I brush my teeth and get ready for bed, I knock on Chevelle's door.

"What?"

"Just... please wear some pajamas tonight?"

She chuckles softly. "Okay."

The thought of her naked behind that door is too much to bear, but honestly, I think I knocked because I wanted an invitation into her bed.

One time didn't quench my thirst for her in the slightest, which means I'm screwed.

Lying in bed, I pull up the text string with all the Greene brothers.

I don't expect an answer because it's so late, but surprisingly, a bunch comes through.

Cade: I'm busy getting screamed at while Presley has this baby, man.

Fisher: Boys' night. I'm in. I'll get back with Allie's schedule.

Adam: Only during the day. Nights are reserved for the family.

Xavier: I'm in San Fran, man. Won't be home for a while. But you can just video conference me in or something.

Jed: Just make it at Truth or Dare anytime I'm working.

So we have a tentative plan for me to talk to the Greene brothers about dating their baby sister. I wonder if I can reserve one of those blowup sumo suits.

Chapter Seventeen

Chevelle

A week later, we're about to enter Northern Lights Retirement Center. Thankfully, Cam has stopped acting as though I'm pregnant and we must marry for him to do right by me. Although it's awfully hard not to touch him now, knowing exactly what's under his clothes and knowing he knows how to use it.

"You ready for this?" he asks, parking my car.

I was really tired after work and didn't want to drive to Lake Starlight, even if it's not that far away.

We walk into the building, and LeeAnn, the activities coordinator, is behind the counter. "I heard you two got signed up without knowing it."

"It's okay. We're happy to help," Cam says.

"Speak for yourself. I heard they get all dirty."

LeeAnn laughs. "I will admit I've never worked in a home that's quite so open about their sexuality. But this isn't my first home where they're having more sex than me."

We all laugh.

She comes around the counter. "We've set up some stations for them to work at. I don't anticipate them working out for a long time. So, you can just give tips."

We follow her into the recreation room. Sure enough, they have different weights and balls set up.

"I feel very unprepared. I don't want anyone getting hurt. I work out for myself, but I'm not a trainer," I say.

"You'll be fine," LeeAnn says and steps away.

Grandma waves at me conspicuously as if she's my kid on parent career day. I wave back.

"Okay, ladies and gentlemen. For those of you who don't know, this is Chevelle Greene, Ethel's granddaughter, and her friend, Cameron Baker. They're here to continue health and fitness week by teaching you guys how to use small weights to keep up that muscle mass. So please, everyone, be kind and keep inappropriate thoughts to yourself."

"Where do I get an outfit like you?" a woman calls to me.

Cam looks at me, and I look down at myself. I probably could've dressed a tad more conservatively. Tight leggings and a sports bra aren't really appropriate, but it's what I wear when I run or work out.

"I'll be sure to leave links with my grandma where I shop."

"Please, Rita, you'd never look good in that," someone else says.

I hold up my hand. "Hey now, we don't body shame here."

Cam looks at me. "Where do you want to start?"

"Let Chevelle start," Isaac says, pointing at me with his cane.

Cam raises his eyebrows.

"Okay, how about I'll leave the weights to Cam, and I'll teach you more about how to use your own body?"

"Whatever you want to do, sweetheart," Isaac says.

"First, we need to stretch. Everyone, stand if you're able. If you're not, LeeAnn, can you demonstrate from a wheelchair?"

LeeAnn goes and sits in an empty wheelchair.

"Raise your hands in the air, stretching and pressing them toward the ceiling," I say, demonstrating.

"Oh yeah, I feel that," Grandma says. "Good job, Chevelle."

"Thanks, Grandma."

I continue doing the arm stretches, the abdomen stretches, then I bend at the waist. "I know a lot of you can't touch your toes, so just go until you feel the stretch."

"Can you turn around so I can see it better?" Earl asks.

"Seriously?" Cam deadpans.

"What? I have a learning disability. I need to see it from all angles." Earl eyes Cam.

I turn around and bend over. "You can cross your ankles to stretch one side more than the other."

"Man, I already feel my muscles getting hard," Isaac says, and I bolt up.

"Come on, guys," Cam interjects.

"You're the one with the dirty mind, man." Isaac's cane is pointed in Cam's direction.

He and I share a look.

"Okay. Now that we're all stretched out, Cam will show you some exercises with the small weights, and you can each take turns coming up to the station to practice yourselves."

I hand the class over to Cam, who picks up small dumbbells he could probably lift with his pinkie.

"Just so you know, I was a three-time Navy boxing champ," a man says as he approaches Cam. "I could probably pick you up, little lady."

"Let's save that for another day," LeeAnn says.

"I bet you can't do it," he challenges Cam.

I roll my eyes and shake my head. We are not allowing them to lure us into their weird games.

"Let's just concentrate on you. We can do some bicep curls." Cam demonstrates.

Another woman comes over to me. "I walk every day, do squats." She slaps her ass. "Feel it. Rock hard." She smacks her ass again.

I give her a small smile. "I trust you."

"Nonsense." She grabs my hand and places it on her ass. "Squeeze it. See? No fat."

"Great job," I say and rip my hand away.

"Oh please, Olive, that's from all the sex you have. Your ass cheeks are always clenching," Midge calls to the woman.

What is up with these old people?

"Come on, bench press the girl." The Navy guy still isn't letting it go. He reaches for me, and I shoot Cam a panicked look. "I'll show you how it's done if you're so scared."

"Whoa." Cam drops the small weights and removes the man's hand from my waist. "Okay, I'll do it."

"No, you won't," I whisper-shout.

"Unless you want to be the cause of this poor man going to the hospital, I suggest you let me bench press you." He waits with raised eyebrows. I hate when he acts all smug.

"Fine."

We head to the bench area.

"This is fun. Who has a camera?" Dori asks.

"No pictures!" I call as Cam lies on the bench.

He cracks his neck a few times as if he's about to lift the most weight he ever has.

"This is so immature." I shake my head.

"I got a twenty that says he drops her." The Navy guy waves the bill in the air.

"He'll be fine, Wilbur. Do you see those biceps?" Dori says.

"I'm going to have dreams about those biceps. My late

Richard had arms like that," a woman who looks at Cam as though she'd like to eat him says.

"Can we hurry this up?" Cam whispers to me.

"How do you want me? Back or front?"

"I'd like you every way, but right now, let's do one of my hands under your arm and the other on your hip." He stretches his arms a couple times. The longer he takes to prepare to hold me, the less confident I am he can hold me up. "Okay, come on."

I lower myself onto his hands, and one presses into my armpit and the other molds to my hip. My feet rise from the floor, and I'm hovering over him.

"You have to lower her and push her back up." Damn, Wilbur is annoying the shit out of me. He must be a new guy. "Last chance for bets."

A few people rush over to him and hand over twenties. Meanwhile, I feel Cam's hands repositioning underneath me.

"Are you sure you have me?" I whisper.

"Relax. I've got this."

"Don't be too cocky."

He lowers me to his chest, and I close my eyes as he pushes me back up.

"Double or nothing, you can't do it again," Wilbur shouts.

"It's enough, Cam," I say, but I'm already being lowered. "He's a ninety-year-old man. You don't have to prove anything to him."

"Maybe I just like having you in my hands." He laughs, and after he pushes me back up, he bends his body so my feet land on the floor. He sits up and holds up his hands. "Any other challenges?"

Wilbur starts paying out people, ignoring Cam.

"We're always getting off track at these events." LeeAnn shakes her head. "Everyone, go back to a station and wait for instruction."

They all move slowly in silence. Meanwhile, all I can do is stare at Cam because it's sexy as hell that he just bench-pressed me.

"He's a keeper." Olive nudges me with her elbow.

"Oh, we're not..."

Her eyes widen. "Why the hell not? You're young, he's young. Take it from an old lady. Get it while you can. These men are a lot of talk, but that age..." She nods at Cam. "All that testosterone." She's staring at Cam as if he's her favorite dessert and she's been on a lifetime diet.

I don't say anything, stepping away while she gawks at him.

"We should have a wet T-shirt contest next." Earl waggles his eyebrows at me.

"I think we need some fresh air. Let's go for a walk around the pond," LeeAnn announces.

They all groan like a bunch of elementary kids finding out it's indoor recess because it's raining.

We file out and it's still a nice day. The sun is low in the sky but still shining. Cam is intently talking to one of the more attentive men who generally seem interested in learning how to be more in shape.

"Careful of the ducks. They're territorial," LeeAnn reminds everyone.

We're walking on the path around the lake and I'm pushing a nice woman in a wheelchair. Everyone is talking about the weather and how soon we'll be inside for the winter. I wonder whether Cam will still be living with me during the winter months. If he does, we'll be spending a lot more time together. And that scares me because I've seen a different version of him recently.

A duck squawks at Cam as he passes the family, and he looks back. The duck squawks again and steps out of the small brush by the pond onto the track area. Cam walks a little faster.

"Cherish that body," Rita distracts me. "One day, you're going to look in the mirror and wonder what happened."

I smile at her. "I think you're beautiful."

The duck is now on the track and following Cam, who is almost jogging, leaving behind the man he was walking with. "Um... LeeAnn?"

"Just keep walking. They'll turn around soon."

But the duck isn't turning around, only moving faster. Cam's legs transition into a jog.

"It's just a duck, don't be a wuss!" Wilbur screams. "Face him like a man."

"No, no. We don't want anything to happen to the duck." LeeAnn's tone turns frantic.

"Can someone do something?" Cam shouts.

"Back in my day, we'd have that duck by the neck," Wilbur says to the group of goons who follow him.

"We don't harm animals," LeeAnn says.

"Seriously? It's about to peck at me." Cam picks up his knees and goes into a full sprint.

"Oh, he's fast. Hopefully not in the bedroom though." Rita elbows me in the side, and I hold my hand there to stop her from doing it again.

I smile at her, biting down my laughter as Cam runs away from a duck who's half flying, half running to catch him.

"What did I do to it?" Cam asks. "I'm sorry, duck, please leave me the hell alone."

"All those muscles and underneath lies a pussy." Wilbur shakes his head.

"I'd like to see you get a hold of that duck." I challenge him.

He puffs out his chest and stomps toward the area with the other duck families.

"No!" LeeAnn holds out both of her hands.

Cam runs by where the duck's family is, and the other older duck squawks, making the one chasing Cam stop and head back toward his family.

"She must be the wife. Always having to tell her husband to stop being an asshole." Rita shakes her head.

I smile at Cam as he's bent over, trying to regain his breath. He catches my eyes and smiles at me, shaking his head. As though we're having our own nonverbal conversation.

Grandma comes by and pats my hand. "Great job, sweetie."

"Thank you." I kiss her on the cheek.

"He's a good one. Someone you can trust." She wraps her arm around my waist and lays her head on my arm.

I look at Cam. "I know, Grandma. I know."

And I do, but taking that step feels like the first step on a tightrope over the Grand Canyon. One misstep and I might never recover.

Cam

I lost the bet and Rowdy was way too happy to hand over the fish costume I'll have to wear for two hours today. Charters are slow for everyone as the season dwindles down, so we're all hoping some late-season tourists will want to schedule an impromptu fishing trip after seeing me in this ridiculous thing.

As I'm putting it on, my phone dings.

> Fisher: Cam wants to meet us, and I want my basement done. Meet at my house tomorrow at nine am. Everyone is helping. We have shit to do.

We've been trying to figure out a day and time that works for everyone for a week. It's so like Fisher to get annoyed and take control, demanding everyone's participation. And I'm grateful. I want to get this over with. Still, my anxiety picks up from thinking about having to have "the talk" with all of Chevelle's brothers. It's bad enough that I've already slept with her once without asking their permission to date her. She still thinks I'm crazy, but the other night when I brought home dinner for us, I didn't hear her complaining about boundaries. We even shared a blanket while watching a movie.

"Sorry." Chevelle comes over and helps me with the costume. "I suddenly feel guilty about hiding that fish and getting your charter drunk."

"Don't forget the laxative." I raise an eyebrow.

"Eh... that I don't feel bad about. That girl was all over you."

She can't see the smile on my face since my head is in the fish costume already. And I'm not going to call her out on why it bothered her. We weren't a couple—strike that, *aren't* a couple. But Chevelle likes me and it's not just a little girl crush like when we were younger. She's softening to me.

"I think I'm going to throw up." I cough.

"I know. It's like someone soaked it in fish guts or something."

"Not helping." I cough again. "Jesus, what the hell?"

"It's just two hours." She takes my hand and guides me out of the marina since it's hard to see all the way to the ground in this thing. "It'll go by in a flash. Don't worry."

"I won't complain if you want to bathe me afterward?"

She lightly smacks my back. "Yeah, okay. Now use that charming personality to get us some charters."

She leaves me on the sidewalk at the entrance to the marina, and it doesn't take long before I have people harassing me.

"Oh, who is this?" Rylan and his buddy Declan come up.

"Keep on walking, little Greene."

"Cam? Is that really you?" Declan tries to look through the breathing screen.

"Shit, man. What'd you do?" Rylan asks and laughs.

"He's probably doing it to get in Chevelle's pants." Declan laughs.

Rylan jabs him in the arm. "Gross, that's my sister, man."

"I lost a bet," I tell them.

"You? I'm shocked." Declan, who I think has always looked up to me for some reason, should be appalled, because I am too.

Declan's parents have money, and they belong to the same club as my parents. His dad is a hotshot lawyer in Anchorage and commutes so his son can live in a nice area. I don't think he realizes that his son is the delinquent of the school.

"Keep it moving, boys." I point down the road.

"Why would we do that when we can be here, harassing you? Besides, we've been trying to think of a senior prank, and I think you're just the man to help us." Declan smacks me on the back.

"My high school days are over. And didn't you guys get into trouble a couple years ago? Breaking and entering?"

"We were amateurs." Rylan laughs.

"You're still amateurs," I say. "Not to mention your brother's the sheriff and your brother-in-law is the mayor. You have way too many people that you're going to piss off." I wish he could see how serious I am, but to them, we're on equal footing. Probably because I don't take much seriously. "Go find something productive to do."

"See you later, Moby," Declan says as the two walk away.

"Why would you say Moby?" Rylan asks.

"You know, from that book," Declan says.

Rylan's head falls back in laughter. "Man, Moby Dick was a whale."

And that's why that kid already has a scholarship to Stanford. Not only is he a soccer god, but the kid's got brains too.

Once they walk down the sidewalk toward whatever trouble they're going to find, I wave at a few cars and take a few pictures with kids, handing out brochures from Chevelle, mine, and Rowdy's charters.

An hour into it, I spot my parents walking back from their lunch. I purposely sidestep to not be in their direct line of sight.

"Oh, I love the fish costume. Did you bring that back?" my mom asks my dad as they approach.

"Yeah, I think it brings the friendly vibe back." He smiles at my mom, and I want to call him out on his lie.

"You haven't demoted our son to that position, have you?" she asks.

"No."

"Are you about done with this little experiment? We both know that you're going to hand him the business," my mom says.

They continue walking, so I pretend I'm waving to someone behind them so I can get closer.

"He's been doing okay on the charters. I wish he'd show more initiative, but I guess I've punished him enough."

"Yes, you have. He's our only son, and you know we're to blame. We gave him anything he ever wanted without him having to work for it." My mom slides her arm through my dad's.

"I'll call him in this week."

They walk toward the marina offices, and I sit on the ledge. I've enjoyed my time out of that office. I never thought I would, but I do. The excursions aren't great, but I love being on the open water, on my own schedule for the most part, and away from my dad.

I really need to figure out what I'm gonna do if I decline his offer to bring me back. There's no maybe in whether I can make it without him. I *have* to make it without him.

Nine o'clock on the dot, I arrive at Fisher's place with my toolbox to help him with his basement. It's the least I can do since I've gone behind his back and slept with his sister. I feel guilty about it, but not as guilty as if it had just been a quick romp I didn't want to lead to anything. Which is exactly why I'm here today.

A few Greene boys' trucks are already in the driveway, so I sit in Chevelle's car she let me borrow and try to gather the nerve to talk to them all. They've known me their entire lives, so there shouldn't be a problem with me dating Chevelle, right? Plus, they know how much I protect her, just like they would.

Adam pulls up next to me and gets out of his truck, then looks at me sitting inside the car. "What are you doing?" he asks through the window.

I grab the keys and toolbox, exiting the car. "Nothing. I didn't want to wake the twins."

His forehead scrunches. "Well, the fact that Jed and Cade are already here says they're probably up."

"Yeah, right, of course."

He gives me a funny look, then walks up the steps of his childhood home and looks over his shoulder. "You okay, Cam?"

I nod, wishing I wasn't already sweating when I haven't even taken one swing of my hammer yet.

All the guys used to live in this house together, but one by one, as they found love, they moved out, except for Fisher, who decided he wanted to live here long term with Allie and raise their kids. I have to assume some of the Greenes struggle with being here since just beyond the trees is the small lake where the accident happened with Chevelle and their mom.

Adam walks in the house without knocking.

Allie is on the floor in the living room with Axel and Laurie, trying to get them to interact with some toy. "Boys."

"So, is that a rule, we can just walk in?" I ask.

"Sure, but no complaints when you find us swinging with another couple." Allie eyes Adam. I'm assuming this isn't their first conversation about this.

He cringes. "Hard habit to break. Sorry."

She smiles at him because Allie is too nice for her own good. But I guess that's the difference between her and Fisher. She's sunshine, he's grumpy. It works.

"They're downstairs. I'm just about to take these two to my friend's house in Lake Starlight, so I'll see you guys later," she says.

I see the twins' coats on the floor.

"You'll be having more fun than us." Adam walks toward the basement.

"Do you need help getting them dressed?" I ask.

Adam stops and turns to look at me.

Allie laughs. "Thank you, but I have it."

I follow Adam down the basement stairs, and we find Fisher, Cade, and Jed all sitting on buckets and shooting the shit.

"What the hell is this?" Adam asks.

"We're talking plans before we get started," Fisher says.

There are piles of two-by-fours and drywall in the corner. At least Fisher took care of that.

I'm not sure I can work side by side with them all day without blurting out what I need to talk to them about, so I grab a bucket and sit in their circle. "Good. Can we talk about something else for a second?"

They all look at me, and I feel the weight of their stares like lead on my shoulders.

"You know how I'm staying at Chevelle's, right?"

"Yeah, we're all surprised one of you isn't buried under the back porch," Jed says, and they laugh.

"Actually, we get along pretty well."

They all quiet.

"Heard you lost the bet." Cade elbows me. "He had to wear the fish costume," he tells the rest of them.

"I thought I smelled something." Adam plugs his nose.

I groan but push through because there's no future for Chevelle and me until I get their approval.

"I like your sister, and I want to date Chevelle." The words fall out of my mouth like vomit.

The laughter comes to an abrupt stop, and four pairs of eyes drill into me.

Now, I've given this a lot of thought, and I don't think Jed will fight it. They're stepsiblings, and he's really easygoing. Plus, he wasn't the settling down type either, so he'll understand how a man can change when he meets the right woman. Adam will probably just go with whatever the consensus is. I'm most worried about Fisher and Cade. After the accident, all the brothers took responsibility for watching out for Chevelle, but Fisher and Cade even more so than the rest. And Xavier...

"Actually, hang on." I pull out my phone and dial Xavier.

He answers, and his voice is groggy from sleep. "Do you know what time it is?" There are some muffled noises. "It's Cam," he says to who I assume is Clara.

"I'm putting you on speaker," I say. "We're at Fisher's, and all your brothers are here. I've just told them that I want to date Chevelle. I want all of your blessings."

"Are you already dating?" Adam asks, the line between his eyebrows deepening.

I shake my head. "No, I wanted you all to be okay with it before I ask her out."

Xavier groans, but I hear movement too. "I'll be back, baby."

"You think you have a shot at Chevelle?" Jed laughs. "I hate to break it to you, man, but she hates you."

Hates me enough to fuck me. They don't get how much has changed with us and how much we've both been hiding our feelings for the past few years.

I shake my head. "No, she doesn't. I think she'll be receptive to it. But like I said, I need you guys to be okay with it first."

Cade looks up at me from under his eyebrows. "I don't wanna be a dick, but she's not going to date you."

"Is there something we don't know?" Fisher asks, voice stern.

I adamantly shake my head. "No."

The last thing I want Fisher to know is that I took his sister on the table of my boat and didn't respect her enough to even give her a bed for our first time together.

Adam smacks me on the back. "Good luck, and make sure you wear a cup when you ask her." He goes over to the old fridge in the corner and grabs a water.

Jed stands. "I feel like I should do some sort of a blessing on you. Good luck."

That leaves Cade and Fisher. Fisher doesn't look happy, but then he stands too. "If she says yes, then I'll change the twins' poopy diapers for a month. Sorry, buddy, but I think you're reading mixed signals. But if by some fucking miracle she agrees, you'd better show her the respect she deserves and if you hurt her... we got a problem, am I clear?"

"Speaking from experience," Xavier says through the phone, "I know what it's like to go from friends to enemies to lovers, so I hope it works out the way you want it to. I think we can all agree that we just want them both to be happy."

There's a murmur of agreement from the rest of the guys.

Cade remains sitting on the bucket. He's the only one who hasn't given his opinion yet. He's the eldest of the family, besides Jed, but Jed is from Marla's side. "I've always appreciated how much you protect Chevelle, but let me give you a little advice when it comes to her. I think where you go wrong is that Chevelle doesn't want someone to protect her. She lives her life how she wants and doesn't want anyone's opinion on it. I'm cool if you ask her out because I'm sure she can handle herself and I know she won't feel obligated to say yes, but if she does agree, it'll never work if you intend on telling her what to wear, who she can talk to. Don't big brother her." He stands. "Twenty says she says no." He pulls out his wallet.

The other brothers continue to razz me, saying I have no shot with their sister, but I'll prove them wrong. I'm going to prove to her I'm worthy, and they'll all be eating their words. The best news is that I'm leaving here without any blatant nos, and I say that gives me the green light.

Chevelle

I decide to stop at The Grind to get a coffee and talk with Zoe. She was my mom's best friend, and they owned this place together until my dad signed over my mom's portion to Zoe. She's always been sort of like a mom to me. Well, before Marla came into the picture. I love Marla too, but Zoe knew my mom. Knew her thoughts, her dreams.

After the rush is gone, she sits down with me at a table. "So, what's up?"

I shrug.

Her foot nudges mine under the table. "Chevelle?"

"Am I just scarred beyond repair?"

She laughs until she realizes I'm serious, then she quickly sobers. "Sweetie, not at all. Why would you think that?"

"You know Cameron Baker, right?"

She smiles. "Who doesn't?"

Which is true. Everyone around here knows his family, even without his "never met a stranger" personality.

"Did you know he's staying with me?" I ask.

"I own the coffee shop. I know everything that goes on in town."

She's right. It only took me one summer of working here

in high school to realize everyone keeps talking while their barista prepares their coffee. It's like they think we can't hear over the machines or something.

"Anyway, things are different between us now."

"I always thought you didn't like him."

I sip my coffee and look at her over the rim of my cup. Whatever she sees, she slides back in her chair and nods. See? It's like she's got motherly senses. At least when it comes to me.

"It's the classic story of crushing on your brother's best friend." I shrug.

"Like when boys are mean to girls on the playground when they really like them?" she asks, smiling.

"Kind of. But I think I've always crushed on him because he sees it."

"Sees what?" Zoe asks, looking at the door when the bell rings.

I glance over my shoulder, but it's just a woman meeting another woman who ordered her a coffee already. "He sees me."

"We all see you, Chevelle." She reaches across the table and squeezes my hand.

"He sees my pain, and he wants to help heal me. Heal my pain."

She sighs again. No one ever wants to talk to me about my mom's death or the fact that she wouldn't have been on that ice had I not wandered off looking for my brothers. She'd be the one I'd be talking to right now. And I wouldn't be scared of Cam and his intentions. I'd be excited. Everyone but Cam is under the belief that therapy fixed me. And it helped for sure, but there are some things I think you always carry with you, and this is one.

"Can I admit something to you?" she asks.

I nod.

"Craig healed me. I was still in mourning over your mom, fearful of getting close to someone and seeing them taken away again. Your mom was my best friend, my business partner, and I never wanted to trust another person with my heart after I lost her. But I did, and I'm so happy with Craig."

"But you didn't kill her."

A strangled noise comes from deep in her throat. "Chevelle." There are those sympathetic eyes again.

I shake my head. "It's okay, I don't... I mean, I'll always have my what-ifs. But it's not on a daily basis like when I was little."

She sighs. "You like him though?" She doesn't continue the conversation about my mom because she knows she'll get nowhere there.

"Yeah. I'm not sure I'm ready yet though."

"Then you give yourself some time. If he really likes you and wants something long term, then he needs to understand that you need time."

The bell rings, and from the sound of the number of people, I know Zoe's gotta go help them. She gives me a look to ask if I'm okay.

"I'm good. You go." I wave her off.

She leaves me, and I sip my coffee. Her radio is playing the local station, and Nikki and Chip's Scandals of Sunrise Bay is replaying from earlier this morning.

"I know everyone sees it, Chip," Nikki says.

"I saw her helping him with the fish costume the other day," Chip adds and I sit up straight in my chair. Was Nikki talking about me on her show? "He's still staying at her place."

"We've all seen them walking to work together, laughing

and enjoying one another's company, when before they used to be at each other's throats. Was it all a facade?" Nikki flares up the dramatics.

"Playground crush?" Chip says.

"I did hear something this morning that I didn't know if I should share here, but I've always promised my listeners the truth. There have only been a few times over the years when I didn't report on something having to do with my family. I won't talk about how Chevelle and Cameron got into the situation they're in, but I do have something to share."

Thank God she's not going to talk about Derek. As the weeks have passed, I feel less and less shaken over what happened and grateful I was able to extricate myself from the situation so quickly, but I don't want everyone talking about it.

"So what's the gossip?" Chip asks as if he's salivating.

"Cam might or might not have sat down with all the Greene brothers and asked for permission to date Chevelle."

My eyes widen and my mouth hangs open. I look around the room, but it's all tourists who don't know that I'm the Chevelle my stepsister Nikki is talking about.

"Bye, Zoe." I wave and dispose of my coffee on the tray she has by the trash can.

Everything I just said about Cam vanishes from my mind because he does not get to go ask permission from my brothers. I'm my own person.

Ugh, that man pisses me off.

I SLAM the front door and Cam peeks his head out from the

kitchen. He's wearing an apron and holding a wooden spoon.

I narrow my eyes. "Where do you get off involving my brothers in my business?"

He steps out of the kitchen. "I told you I had to ask their permission to date you."

I throw my hands in the air. "There is no dating going on between us. I was clear. The sex was a mistake."

He disappears into the kitchen again and comes out without the wooden spoon but has the apron on. "I think you need to stop denying what's happening here."

I strip off my light jacket and put it on the coat hanger. Then I untie my boots and put them by the door. "There isn't anything happening here. You've had sex before. What happened on that boat was just sex."

His jaw tightens. "Bullshit."

I clench my fists and glare at the ceiling. "From now on, leave you and me out of your mouth when you're with my brothers. We were on Scandals of Sunrise Bay!" I throw out my arms again.

"I respect your brothers too much to not go to them."

I walk by him into the living room, but he swings his arm around and grabs me by my waist.

"When are you going to stop denying this?"

I struggle to get out of his grip, and he allows me. "There is nothing here."

"Come on, I made you dinner. Let's sit and talk. Want to make a pro and con list?"

"A pro and con list?" I ask with my eyes crinkling. What is his deal?

"If you're not going to listen to what your body and heart are telling you, we can look at the facts."

"What do you not understand? I'm mad at you right now.

You went to my brothers to ask permission. This isn't the eighteenth century, Cam. I make my own decisions."

He widens his stance and unties his apron. "I'm not apologizing for what I did. Your brothers are like my brothers. I'm not going to blindside them." He tosses the apron on the couch. "Dinner's ready."

He walks by me, but this time it's my hand grabbing his. He doesn't look back at me, still facing the stairs.

"I know," I say. "But I don't ask my brothers' permission when it comes to decisions I make in my life."

"You don't have to, but I do." He glances over his shoulder, then finally turns around. He takes my hand, threading our fingers together.

"What if they'd said no?"

"Then I would've talked them into it. I'm not saying I wouldn't have done anything with you, but I would have fought for this."

I look up and his piercing eyes reveal so much emotion, I become lost.

He inches closer, his hand cradling my cheek, and I tilt my head, pressing into his palm. "I can't apologize for what I did, but their decision wasn't going to be the end of us."

"Cam?"

"Yeah," he whispers.

I inch closer and rise on my tiptoes, placing my lips on his. His hand tightens on the side of my face, keeping me in place. Our kiss starts gentle and sweet, but his other hand comes up and holds the other side of my face. His tongue licks the seam of my lips, and I open for him.

With our bodies flush to one another, I wrap my arms around his neck. He moves his hands to my waist, walking me backward, and I fall over the arm of the couch. I laugh, staring up at him. He strips off his shirt and tosses it on the chair, looking at me with a heated gaze that makes me ache between my legs.

"You want this?" he asks with a tone that says if I say no, he might just die right here.

"You don't have to ask me."

He unbuttons my pants and lowers my zipper. "Until you're mine, I do."

I lift my ass off the couch, and he pulls my pants and panties down my legs, tossing them in a pile with his shirt. He swings my legs over his shoulders and drags his knuckle down my center. A million electric currents rush through my body at the same time.

"So wet already," he says and lowers his mouth to my pussy.

My fingers weave through his hair, gripping it when his tongue twirls my clit. The man knows what he's doing down there, and my head falls onto the soft cushion, my hips rocking up and down, desperate for the friction of his mouth to take me to a place I've rarely gone before with a partner.

With Cam, I lose myself, my inhibitions, and my doubts. No man has ever made me feel as wanton as he does. No man has ever made me *feel* as much as him, period.

His finger teases my opening while his mouth concentrates on my clit. When he plunges one finger inside me, my ass rises off the couch and a moan slips from his mouth.

"God, Cam."

He looks at me, and our eyes lock, a smirk on his lips. That cocky side of him is evident even while he pleasures me.

Another finger pushes inside me, and he arches it to hit my G-spot. That's all it takes before I lose control and I'm grinding on his face, taking my pleasure into my own hands.

He continues to push and slide his fingers in and out of me. My orgasm comes like a flash flood, and I feel as though I'm tumbling through the rapids until it calms, then I'm floating on the water in post-orgasm bliss.

He pulls his fingers out of me and licks them clean while staring at me. I sit up straight and undo the button of his pants. While I fiddle with them, he gets me free of my shirt. Soon we're both naked.

"We're moving this upstairs." He carries me upstairs and deposits me on the bed. Going to his drawer, he pulls out a condom.

I take it from his hand and push him down on his back. "I'm taking control this time."

He lies with his arms behind his head. "No complaints here."

And there aren't any complaints when I take his base and sink down on his incredible length. His hands hold my hips, but he allows me to dictate the pace. I come again before he flips me over and thrusts inside me from behind.

This man knows how to pleasure a woman, and by the end, I'm a sated mess sprawled out on his bed. I don't know what to think when I realize I wouldn't want to be anywhere else in that moment.

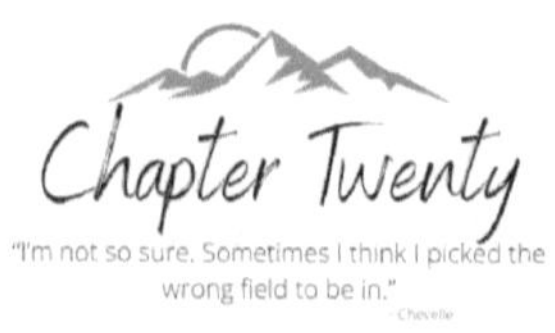

Chapter Twenty

Chevelle

The evening excursions always have a little more of a party vibe. Especially the bachelor parties.

I see Cam sitting in his boat, watching as tonight's guys walk toward my boat. There are six of them, and they've clearly already been drinking. Cam eyes me and goes back to watching them.

His own excursion group is getting settled in his boat. A group of three couples who probably won't even fish. Sure, the guys will put their rods in, but the women will sit up front and sip their wine and gawk at Cam. He's got another guy, Gage, on the boat because Cam knows he'll be torn in two different directions. That's the problem with luxury fishing boats like his—they demand a higher level of service, which means more staff.

"Welcome to Reelaxing Fishing Tours," I say to the guys.

They each look me up and down. I'm used to that. It's not a big deal. I've never felt like I couldn't handle myself.

"Are you the entertainment?" one guy asks.

I instinctively look at Cam, although he's far enough away that he didn't hear what they said. "No. I'm your tour guide."

"Shit. Really? Girls like you fish? Hell, who's the lucky

bastard who got you?" The one guy doesn't stop talking the entire time he boards.

Another guy gives me a look of apology, but he's holding a fifth of alcohol, which means I don't trust him.

Once everyone is boarded, I catch sight of Cam getting his boat ready as well.

"Let's go over safety," I say.

"It's fine." One guy waves me off.

"I swam in college," another says.

"Regardless of your swimming skills and whether you've been on a fishing boat before, the life jackets are under the bench. There is enough for all of us. Should you want to wear one the whole time, you are more than welcome. Please do not put your hands or any other body part out of the boat while we're moving. Once we're anchored, you may move around. There are drinks in the coolers, and I'll put out the food when we stop. The excursion will last two hours and fifteen minutes, then we'll head back to the marina during the remaining fifteen minutes. Are there any questions?"

One guy raises his hand. "Are you this bossy in bed?"

Trying to keep it light, I wink and say, "Only my boyfriend knows the answer to that."

They all say "ohhh" in unison.

"Then let's get started. Please remain seated while I get us to where we're going to fish."

I go to my wheelhouse and start the engine, then navigate out of the marina. Cam's already ahead of us. For some reason, I thought he was going to wait for me because he was worried, and then I was going to give him a piece of my mind.

When we get to open water, he turns to the right, and I go to the left to head toward Sandcastle Island. It's an island that's not habitable, but a lot of boats stop for their guests to walk in the water and even swim. There's a good fishing spot, and if it ends up being bad, I figure this group won't mind partying there.

The guys all continue to drink on the way to our destination, and I'm pretty sure they're talking about me since every once in a while, one of them looks my way. Other than that, they seem harmless, although not one of them is wearing a wedding ring. I like the married guys better because they usually treat me with more respect.

I cut the motor when we reach our destination, and we glide to a spot I've had success with in the past. After tossing the anchor down, I get the poles ready and pull out the bait. "Okay, guys. Does anyone need help?"

"Oh no, we're all skilled," one guy with a cocky attitude says. I can read the innuendo in the way he says it that we're not talking about the same thing.

Everything is good for about forty-five minutes. Mostly because these guys are struggling to get their bait on because they've all drank way too much. After I've gone around like a kindergarten teacher and helped each one, they sit back and relax, waiting for the fish to snatch the bait.

I bring out the food, but none of them are interested in eating.

One of them falls asleep and the rest decide to draw on his face. I roll my eyes because I hate these charters. These are the ones where I'm thankful I have a gun in the locked box.

"This is boring. Did you say something about an island?" the bald guy says.

"Yes." I glance at my watch. "But we wouldn't have much time there."

"Better than this." He stands and steps on the edge of the boat. "To the island."

"Please get down before you fall."

Thankfully, he listens. I bring up the anchor and start the motor. One of the guys helps me collect the rods, and I hang them from the back of my boat.

When we arrive, the island is crowded because it's a Saturday night and you never know, this could be the last warm weekend of the season. One of the guys runs and jumps out of my boat before I can drop anchor.

"Don't do that again," I call to him.

He just laughs and walks up the sand, approaching the first woman he sees.

They each file out with their beers in hand and walk the island while I wait in the boat. I'm busy on my phone, and when it's time to leave, and they haven't returned, I hop off the boat in search of them.

They're scattered along the beach, some swimming, one making out with a girl, two more tossing a football. I wonder where it came from until I see a pouting kid on the ground near them.

"This group is horrible," I murmur to myself. "Reelaxing Fishing Tours is leaving now. So if you came with Reelaxing Fishing Tours, get back to the boat now. Otherwise you'll be left here." I yell it loudly enough for them to all hear, but none of them come. This is what I was afraid of.

I walk back to the boat and find two of the guys there, asleep again. So much for them helping me round up their friends. I glance at my watch. We're now five minutes late. Another guy stumbles over and says the other three are on their way, but when the other three join us, they have three girls tagging along.

"I'm sorry, just the charter guests are allowed on board.

If you'd like to meet up with them, I'm dropping them in Sunrise Bay."

The girls all look at me as though I ruined their night.

"Come on. Loosen up a bit. I thought you were gonna be a fun one," the guy says and falls face-first on the boat. Blood splatters. I'm pretty sure he might have broken his nose.

He gets up and laughs, as do his two friends.

"Holy shit!" one of the girls cries.

I grab my first aid kit and help the guy get control of his bleeding. Thankfully it's just a cut, not a broken nose.

"We just have to pour alcohol on it." His friend tips a bottle of vodka over his face, and it spills all over my boat.

I close my eyes and suck in a deep breath.

"Here." The bald guy, who I think is the one who booked me, pulls out a wad of cash. "How much to keep this party going?"

"More than you have. I'm taking you guys back, and you can party at the bars in Sunrise Bay."

"But what about our friends?" Another guy swings his arm around one of the girls.

"Sorry, no guests."

"This is bullshit. Who made you chief of the fucking ocean?"

"Sorry, girls," I say and shake my head. They back up, and I grab the rope to free us from the shoreline.

As I push the boat out a little, the bald guy gets behind the wheel. "I'm the captain now." He lets a maniacal laugh loose.

"Get away from the wheel." I jump on my boat and force him aside.

I stare at the radio. Cam's only one call away, but I really don't want to hear, "I told you so" or "you shouldn't be out with all guys." There are plenty of charters that don't act like this.

Then one of the guys jumps off the boat to go rejoin the party on the island. I just need to get them all back to the dock safely.

I pick up the radio. "Cam. Cam. You there? This is Chevelle. Over."

"Cam to Chevelle. Over." Hearing his voice feels like a blanket of calm wrapping around me.

"I need a little assistance here. Do you mind swinging by Sandcastle Island? Over."

"ETA three minutes. Over."

I bring the boat back up to the shore, and the guy who jumped in the water gets back in. So far I have two passed out, one bleeding, one soaking wet. Good times.

Cam shows up, takes one look at the state of the guys, and climbs aboard from his boat. "Think you can get the boat back to the slip in one piece, Gage?"

The guy nods.

"I hate to leave you, ladies and gentlemen, but you're in great hands with Gage. I promise he can multitask, ladies, and keep those wineglasses filled." He winks and all the women sigh. Everyone always loves Cam.

Gage drives off and Cam looks at the guys.

"You're the guy from the other boat," one says.

"Hey, Einstein. Mind getting in an actual seat?" After the guy sits, Cam crosses his arms and sits down with them.

I take us all back to the dock. Once I get us in position next to the dock, Cam jumps out and ropes up my boat. He escorts the guys out of the marina. I'm not sure what he says, but they look slightly chagrined when they leave.

When Cam returns, he doesn't say anything about them, just helps me clean up the mess.

After what feels like a lifetime, I finally blurt, "You can say it."

He looks at me with his forehead wrinkled. "What?"

"I told you so. You've warned me a million times I couldn't handle them on my own."

He sits on my bench seat and pats the spot next to him. "Chevelle, they didn't respect you. Who's to say they would have respected any captain?" He shrugs. "It's not your fault. And I would never tell you I told you so. All I want is for you to be safe out there."

"Thank you."

We look over and see Gage bringing Cam's boat into the marina. "You don't have to thank me. I'm just glad you called me. There was a time you wouldn't have."

I hate that he's right, but he is. I'm surprised myself. And that shows how much we're changing. How I'm trusting him, and man, that scares me.

"Now, you can pay me back by coming somewhere with me tomorrow."

"Okaaay," I say, unsure where he wants to take me. "But first, I'll help you clean your boat."

We leave my boat and head to his.

"And we keep this to ourselves?"

He laughs and puts his arm around my shoulders. "I wouldn't ruin your tough-ass reputation. You earned that fair and square. Like I said, what happened could've happened to anyone."

"I'm not so sure. Sometimes I think I picked the wrong field to be in."

He stops and turns to me, putting his hands on my shoulders. "Do you love it?"

I nod.

"Like you can't imagine doing anything else?"

"For the most part. I love being able to work outdoors and being with different people every day. It's only times like tonight…"

He shakes his head. "Then you keep doing it and love it. Cases like this are rare, and you can call me anytime. I'll always come." He dips his head to my eye level. "And you'll never hear me tell you I told you so. Ever."

I nod, and he seems satisfied as he strides off toward his boat.

My heart thumps, and a feeling I haven't felt in so long washes over me. That crush is transforming into love. I'm sliding down a hill, and I can't gain traction as I fall head over heels in love with Cam. I just hope I'm not on my way to heartbreak along with it.

Cam

Chevelle didn't run away after we had another impromptu sex session last night when we returned home from the marina. In fact, she put on a pair of boxers and a T-shirt, and we got something to eat, talked about our day, Nikki's need to spread gossip, and she complimented me on my cooking skills. I guess everyone assumes I can't cook worth a damn because I'm a bachelor. Everyone in town has assumptions about the guy they think I am.

Which is why I've decided that if I want Chevelle to open up and trust me, I need to do the same. So, I'm taking her somewhere special to me. Somewhere no one else knows about.

"Do you mind if I drive?" I ask for her keys after we're both home and showered.

She hands them over. "Want to blindfold me too?"

I wink. "That's for later."

She laughs, and I swear it's the best sound in the world.

We drive twenty-five minutes to the place in Winterberry Falls. It's by their marina and the only place I could use a fake name and hope no one would recognize me.

I take her hand when we're both out of the car. I love the feel of her soft palm against mine. We're not a couple yet, I know that, but as long as I take things slow with her, I see us getting there.

"Winterberry Falls, huh?"

"I couldn't do this in Sunrise Bay. My dad and... too many people who know who I am." I open the side door of the warehouse and lead us inside. "Hold on, I'll get the lights." I walk over to the switch and turn on the lights.

She stares ahead at the half-finished boat in the center of the large space. This one hasn't been painted yet and the company name isn't on it either. But it's a wooden boat that's being restored, so I'm sure she'll link the two things together. She slowly walks toward the boat, and I watch carefully for her reaction.

"What is this place?" she asks, and I try not to be crushed that she doesn't assume it's mine right away.

In Sunrise Bay, I'm a white-collar guy. The one who doesn't work with his hands. Born rich and will stay rich because of his father's success. For a long time, I was okay with that, hiding behind my ability to make anyone laugh and get any girl I wanted. But a couple years ago, I knew I didn't want to live up to the expectation everyone had for me.

"It's Five Seas' headquarters," I answer.

She looks at me. "This is the mystery boat place? Is this one of the boats?"

I nod. "Will be. It's not finished."

She studies me for a minute, glances back at the boat, and back at me. "Is this yours, Cam? Are you the owner of Five Seas?"

"Not just the owner. I restore them."

Her eyes widen and she walks over to the pictures and drawings pinned to a wall. "Seriously?"

"I know, not what you would expect from me."

She shakes her head. "That's not it. I just... why did you keep it a secret? The boats are beautiful."

I sit on a stool and lean forward, resting my forearms on my thighs. "Insecurity. Judgment. I'm not sure I could've heard someone say anything bad about my idea. I even have a guy who sells them for me, so my name isn't on anything."

Her fingers trace over the purple paint sample on the wall.

"What were you worried about?" She turns and faces me but stays across the room, the boat between us.

"It's the first time I put myself out there. Tried something *I* wanted to do. The first boat was just for me. I wasn't even gonna sell it until I had it on a test drive and everyone who saw it was asking about it when I came back to the dock. Then I thought that maybe this could be more than a hobby."

"People talk about them all the time. Every time I see one, I can't take my eyes off it."

I smile. "Thanks."

"But everyone should know this is you." She walks toward me, rounding the boat. "You're so talented."

"Don't act like you don't know what people think of me in Sunrise Bay. I'm just a rich kid who people think can't do anything. They probably think I hire someone to replace my light bulbs."

She laughs. "I don't think people think that at all. Everyone loves you."

I shake my head. "You're being nice. I started this on a whim, but I think I want to make a business out of it."

"That's great." She walks closer.

I hold my hand out for her, unsure if she'll take it. She places her hand in mine, and I pull her closer, situating her between my legs. "There's something you need to know."

"What?"

I swallow hard. "The name…"

"Five Seas?"

"Yeah."

She tilts her head.

"You're the fifth child, Chevelle. And Chevelle starts with a C."

"What?" Her mouth hangs slightly agape, her eyes wide.

"The purple stripe is the same color of the dress you wore when you were five, at your mother's wake."

She lets out a long breath and steps back, turning her back to me. "Cameron?"

She rarely calls me by my full name, and I covet the sound of it on her lips. Her head shakes as though she can't believe what I'm telling her.

"It's not just since we moved in together, Chevelle. I've had feelings for you for a long time. And I processed them by being overprotective and overbearing and, more recently, telling people I was your boyfriend. I didn't know how Fisher would feel, and he and I have been friends for so long. The minute I saw that bruise on your cheek, I couldn't continue to take a back seat. I'm not even sure what I was waiting for." I stand from the stool and come up behind her. "I was stupid for waiting as long as I did, and maybe if I didn't, you wouldn't have had to endure a guy like Derek who hit you."

I don't touch her because I don't want to startle her. She needs to process this information.

"Don't blame yourself," she softly says. "It's no one's fault but his."

"Do you think I'm a creep?" I whisper.

She slowly turns to face me. "Not at all. It's sweet… it's… it's the most amazing thing anyone has ever done for me."

I cradle her face in my palms. "I don't even know when my feelings progressed, but..."

She covers my hand with hers. "Me either. I guess we can't deny them anymore."

I lower my head and kiss her. Before it gets heated, I pull back because that's not what this moment is supposed to be about. I want her to know it's not her body I want, it's her—her heart and her soul.

Don't get me wrong, I love her body, but it's the way she keeps her brothers in check when they mess up. The way she makes sure to keep her mom's memory alive. The fact she came in here and didn't judge me, only encouraged me.

"So, is that a yes?" I murmur against her lips.

"A yes to what?"

"To dating me, of course." I smirk at her.

She smiles and stares me in the eye. "Do you ever not get what you want, Cameron Baker?"

I shrug. "Rarely."

"Well." She steps back from me and turns to look at the boat. My hands fall to my sides. "It all depends. What are your plans for this endeavor you've started?"

"Why?"

"Because I deserve a man who chases after his dreams." She smiles at me over her shoulder.

"What are you implying?"

She runs a hand over the boat. "You can't do this and run a fishing charter business."

"Clearly. This last month, I've gotten nowhere on this boat. Of course, I have been busy chasing a hot blonde."

She points at me. "I like that answer."

"That was my intention." I watch her walk around and soak in the details.

"So?" She turns around at my table and places her hands on either side of her. "When do you tell your father?"

I balk. Although I want to tell him, getting rid of the security that comes with working for my father and inheriting the marina is scary as hell. "You'd have a very different life with me if I stay the course and take over the marina."

"I would. But I'm just a fisherwoman." She shrugs. "I don't want fancy things."

I want to comment on the fact that Chevelle is openly talking about a future with me so soon after we've just agreed to date, but I'm afraid if I do, I'll spook her. Hell, I'm kinda shocked that I'm not spooked, but something about this conversation feels almost inevitable.

"You'd never have to worry about money again."

She nods. "But I'd have an unhappy partner, and that's a crappy life."

I sit back down on the stool. "I really want this, Chevelle. So much it scares me."

She walks over to me and runs her hands up my thighs, separating them for her to fit between. "There's nothing to be scared about. You already have a success on your hands."

Leaving my father is final. There's no going back after if this new venture doesn't work out.

"I'm right here, next to you. As a friend."

I frown a bit at the word friend. "And?"

"Let's just take this slowly."

I bark out a laugh. "A second ago, you were talking about our life together."

She kisses my cheek. "I was just saying the type of man I want to be with when I'm ready."

"Good to know."

"I thought it was pertinent information. And Cam?"

I run my hands down her hair, studying her face and her features. "What?"

"Thank you. It means a lot to me that you remember the dress I wore and the fact that you named your company after me. More than I can really say."

I pull her into my chest. "You never have to thank me for loving you, Chevelle." She stiffens in my arms. "I'm not saying I'm in love with you. I'm saying I've loved you since the day of your mom's wake. All I wanted to do that day was shelter you from the pain and protect you. I'd never felt that for anyone before. That's when I knew you were someone important in my life." Her body weakens in my hold, and I kiss her temple. "Hungry?"

"Starved."

"Let's eat out here in Winterberry Falls, where no one knows us."

"Sounds perfect."

We leave the warehouse, and I lock it up. We drive over to a food truck circle with five different trucks and order something from each one before sitting at a picnic table to enjoy our food.

It's a little chilly, and it's getting dark, but the string of lights that hang from tree to tree creates the perfect ambience for a first date. Although I'm not labeling our night together. I'm just happy to be spending time with Chevelle and building on what we have, whether we call it a date or not.

Now I need to tell my dad I'm no longer coming back to work for him. Plus, I have to buy myself a car. Maybe he'll give me back my jeep if I pay him for it.

"So, does this mean you're out of the fishing excursion business?" she asks before biting into a taco.

"Yeah. I'll finish out the reservations I have, but no more competition between us."

"It was fun though."

"It was."

We finish eating and walk back to the car holding hands.

"I forgot to ask you what my brothers said when you went to them. Not that it matters. I just wondered."

I chuckle. "Well, they didn't think I stood a chance with you. They're all betting against me."

I open the passenger door, and she turns and slides her arms around my neck. "Fools." She kisses me.

"Definite fools."

I drive us home, and walking into the house with her feels different this time. Why didn't I show her that boat a long time ago? But a part of me realizes, with Chevelle, it's baby steps. We're not fully there yet, but every day we're growing closer. Even if I don't get to call her mine until the last days of my life, she'd be worth it.

Cam

I haven't ridden the elevator of the marina in well over a month. I debated on making an appointment with my father, but then he would've twisted this meeting to suit his own agenda.

Lucky for me, his assistant is out to lunch, so I knock on his office door. He never leaves his office for lunch unless my mom pulls him away.

"Come in," he says.

I open the door, and he doesn't look up right away. Even after his first glance, he looks down before leaning back in his chair and looking me in the eye. He takes off his glasses and tosses them on the desk.

"Cameron," he says my name with curiosity.

Most would never imagine we're father and son from our interactions. I didn't learn how to play football from him; I learned it from Hank Greene when he coached our peewee league. Dad's never even thrown a ball with me or taught me to ride a bike or how to fish. Every time I asked him to spend time with me, he'd say he was setting up my future, which is what makes this conversation so nerve racking.

That's what I meant when I told Chevelle her brothers are like my brothers. The Greenes are my family. And her dad is my second dad.

"Hey, Dad."

"I'm actually glad you came. I was talking to your mother the other day. I'm pretty happy with how the fishing excursions are going." He shuffles through some papers. My dad is familiar with a computer and has one on his desk, but he rarely uses it. Instead, he relies on paper reports. Says he likes to mark them up. "Have a seat."

"I'd like to start, if you don't mind." I take a seat, but I don't lean back because he might kick me out as soon as I tell him why I'm here. No point in getting comfortable.

He holds his hand out to me to start.

"I appreciate all you've done for me over the years." I swallow.

"You're my son. You're blood. I knew working down there would get you to appreciate all I've done."

I try not to roll my eyes because I appreciated it before he sent me down to work on the luxury boat he gifted me. Does he even hear himself talk?

"But... I've found something I really love to do, and I'm going to step away from Baker Corporation and explore my own interests."

"Step away?" he asks with a tilt of his head.

"Yeah." I nod as if he can't hear me.

"You don't want to run the company?"

I shake my head.

He stares at me in confusion. "You don't want the company?"

"I'm sorry." I hold up my hands. "I always thought I did, but you were right. I had to learn something for myself. I need to start from scratch, appreciate the hard work it's gonna take to get my business off the ground."

"And what is this ridiculous business you're starting? Let me guess, it has something to do with a Greene?"

That's one problem my dad always has. He thinks the Greenes somehow stole me away from him, but all they did was include me. Ever since I was little, I was asked to stay for dinner, sleepovers, and even family outings. I was like Hank's sixth kid for the most part, and if not for them, my childhood would've been really lonely.

"You know the boats you've seen around? The Five Seas ones with the purple stripe?"

He draws his head back.

"Those are mine. I restored them."

Again, he stares at me, his jaw tight. "People have been inquiring. Everyone assumed it was one of our businesses."

"It started as a hobby and it just kind of grew from there. I love doing it, but I wasn't sure I could make enough money to make a living at it. I think I can though, now that I've done a few and know what I need to put into them and how much I can charge when I sell them."

"I mean, you have an empire here, ready and waiting for you."

This is where I assumed this conversation would go.

"I know, but I don't want to work in an office and have to be the person people hate because I control their income."

"Are you suggesting people hate me?" He's clearly offended. I guess when you sit in your ivory tower, you don't hear the grumbles from below.

"You're the boss. Who likes the boss?"

He says nothing to that, instead turning the conversation in a different direction. "Why don't you work out of Sunrise Bay? We can make The Five Seas part of the Baker family business."

I knew he'd probably pitch the idea, so I'm prepared. "I

want to make a go of it myself. I don't want to feel like you're standing over my shoulder, questioning my decisions or wondering why it's been a lean month if things don't continue to go well. I need to do this on my own."

"So you're just leaving." He throws his hands up.

I nod. "It's what makes me happy."

"It's hard to be happy with no money, Cameron."

I shrug. "I did well on the first and second boat. But I learned a lot this month, what I need to do to spread the word and make a name for myself."

He nods over and over again.

"Gage can take over the excursions if you want. He did a great job the other night."

He continues to nod without speaking a word.

"Then I'm going to go." I thumb behind me toward the door.

"Your mother will be disappointed. She always loved that this company would be passed down to you and then your own son someday. But I suppose a few wooden boats will be the same for your son, right?"

I stand, not willing to listen to him degrade me. He's the reason I didn't believe in myself at first. The fact I kept my company hidden for this long. But I'm not going to allow him to control me anymore. "If I'm blessed to have a son, I hope he finds what he loves, and I'll do what I can to nurture that love."

My dad's forehead creases. "What does that mean?"

I shake my head. Even if I went off right now and told him everything I feel, in the end, he'd still blame me for being ungrateful. "Nothing. Thank you for everything."

"Hold on." He digs in his drawer, pulls out an envelope, and grabs a set of keys from inside. "Here." He tosses them at me. "The keys to your jeep and the keys to the storage locker. Your salary paid for those things."

It feels so good to have my jeep back. I felt like a loser driving Chevelle's car this entire month. "Thanks."

"Good luck."

I clutch the keys and walk out of his office feeling freer than I ever have. I wish I would've done this ages ago.

ONCE I'M OUTSIDE, I notice Chevelle's boat is docked, but she's not there.

> Where are you?

The three dots appear and disappear, then the text pings.

> I'm at Fisher and Allie's. Babysitting while they go out for a lunch date.

> Okay.

> Did you talk to your dad?

I decide not to message her back but unlock and climb into my jeep. I run my hands along the steering wheel and relish having this little piece of freedom back. It's been way too long.

I can't wait to tell Chevelle and see her reaction when I get to Fisher's. When I get there, I knock on the door.

She whips it open. "They're sleeping," she says through a clenched jaw.

"Oh, sorry," I whisper.

We're quiet as I tiptoe into the house, and she shuts the door.

She looks at the monitor and sighs. "They're still asleep. So to what do I owe this visit?"

I wrap my arms around her waist. There's been more affection between us, but I think I still take her by surprise sometimes. "You have to see how good I am with children. It's the next step for us." I kiss her once.

"Try again," she says.

"I quit. I told my dad everything. And guess what?"

She smiles wide. "What?"

I dangle the keys. "I got my jeep back."

"So you won't be relying on me anymore?" She pretends to pout.

"Now I get to drive you around like a real man." She gives me a bland look, and I chuckle. "Kidding, of course. You can drive me anytime." I wink.

She smacks my arm, then wraps her arms around my neck. "I'm so proud of you. How do you feel?"

My hands travel down her sides. "Fucking fantastic."

"I bet."

I pull her into me, pressing my lips to hers, not waiting to slide my tongue into her mouth. God, she feels good. I lead her backward, kissing her thoroughly. My hands roam her body, and she moans as I nibble on her bottom lip.

"What if..." She glances over my shoulder at the front door.

"Please, they're gonna take their time. We'll just make out a little. No harm." I get her on her back on the couch, and I ease down on top of her. My hand slides up under the hem of her shirt.

Her head falls back and her fingers weave through my hair. I love when she does that. My pants get tighter as I become harder. Maybe just making out was a bad idea, but I want her so badly right now.

We quickly get lost in one another. Before I know it, her shirt is off and she's straddling me. I pull down the cups of her bra, both hands massaging her tits and teasing her nipples with my thumbs. I pinch one, and she arches her back, offering them to me. Who would I be if I denied her the pleasure of my mouth on her tits?

"I love your tits." I take one in my mouth, my tongue swirling around her hard nipple.

Her hand slides down between us, and she rubs my length through my pants. My dick twitches in her hand, desperate to be freed.

The front door opens, and laughter rings out for one second before Chevelle and I still. I look over her shoulder and see a pissed-off Fisher.

"Shit!" I say.

"I didn't hear the car." Chevelle climbs off my lap, holding her arm over her tits and grabbing clothes before running out of the room.

Allie is biting her lip to stop herself from laughing.

"What the fuck, Cam?" Fisher's hands are fisted at his sides.

"What?" I situate myself so Allie doesn't have to see my raging hard-on.

"What the hell are you doing?" The line between Fisher's eyebrows is as deep as I've ever seen it.

"I told you I was gonna pursue her."

Allie raises her eyebrows and leaves the room. She must be in the kitchen because I hear noise coming from there.

"I didn't think she'd actually go for it. Fuck." He pushes his hand through his hair.

Allie peers around the corner. "Language."

"The kids are asleep. Fuck. Fuck. Fuck."

I sit up on the couch. "What? Am I that bad? I'm not good enough for your sister?" I try to keep the hurt from my voice.

He sighs. "No, it's not that. It's just..." Chevelle returns to the room, and he looks at her for a long beat, speaking to her now. "He's my person."

I'm thrown by his words. Fisher isn't an emotional guy. Half the time I don't even know what he's feeling because he's so nonreactive. Sure, I see how he loves Allie and the twins, especially the way he talks about them. But us, we're best friends. I share everything with him. That's the reason I felt it was so important to tell him about Chevelle.

"He's mine too," Chevelle softly admits.

Allie walks out of the kitchen. "Fisher Greene, if you think you're going to sabotage this between them just because you're worried you'll lose Cam if it goes south, we're going to have words. Everyone, come into the kitchen so we can talk about this."

We all follow because as nice as Allie is, she's got a scary side too.

We all sit at the kitchen table, and Chevelle looks at a small box that rests in the middle. "What's this?"

"Just something I found in the basement. I'm trying to get it open, but no one has a key. I think I'm gonna have to drill it."

They're talking about this damn box when really, I just want to get this cleared up.

I look between them both. "I can be both of your people."

"Excuse me?" Allie says and looks at Fisher.

"He's my person," Fisher admits, and Allie teasingly slaps his arm.

"I'm supposed to be your person. I'm your wife!"

He turns to her. "You are. It's just Cam was there when my mom died. I told him everything, and he always understood that if I was quieter, I was thinking of my mom and stuff. But you, you're my person now."

"Sure. Okay." She rolls her eyes.

"But he's that for me too. I guess we could've told you," Chevelle says.

"Hello, I did tell him, and they all blew me off like I didn't have a chance with you." I turn to her. "And look... we're on our way somewhere, right?"

Chevelle takes my hand, threading our fingers together. "I hope you can accept it, Fisher, because regardless of your feelings, I'm going to date Cam."

He pretends to choke on something, and Allie rolls her eyes. "Grow up, Fisher. You're not in high school. Just because you turned a blind eye to their obvious feelings for one another all these years doesn't mean they're not there."

Fisher looks at both of us. "Really? You two like each other? *Like* like?"

I smile at Chevelle. "Definitely *like* like."

She matches my smile. "Totally *like* like."

I kiss her, just a small peck, but Fisher clears his throat. "Can you guys refrain from doing that for a little bit? At least until I get used to this."

"No." I kiss her again, and she giggles. "Now that you guys are home, we're gonna go home too." I stand and offer Chevelle my hand.

"Do we need to talk about this some more?" Fisher says.

"There's nothing to talk about," I say and lead Chevelle out of the house.

Everything is right on track now.

Chapter Twenty-Three

Cam

In the last two weeks, Chevelle and I haven't been extremely public with our relationship, though I think the news has spread. I miss being with her every day since she's out on fishing excursions and I've been working my ass off to get the third boat ready for the water.

The days are hard, but the nights... the nights have been the best nights of my life. Every night we eat dinner together and watch movies on Netflix. The best part is that we go to bed in Chevelle's bed and wake up in each other's arms. We haven't talked again about what the future will bring, and I'm still taking things at a snail's pace so as not to scare her.

Tonight, I want to show her how special she is to me.

"Where are you taking me?" Chevelle holds her hands out in front of her since I have her blindfolded.

"It's a surprise. Hence the blindfold."

"Be careful, I can't see where I'm going. My knee might accidentally hammer into your balls." She stops and moves her leg in the air.

I chuckle and walk us through the marina gate and down to the pier. The keys to the boat are burning a hole in my pocket. Once we get to the third Five Seas boat, sitting in the water, I take off her blindfold.

"Oh, Cam, it's beautiful."

"Not half as beautiful as you."

She gives me a look and rolls her eyes.

"Hey, I've always wanted to use a cheesy line like that. But it's the truth." I pull her to my side and kiss her temple. "Please step aboard."

She slips off her shoes and dangles them from her fingers. "Don't mind if I do."

Holding my hand, she steps down and sits on the bench by the steering wheel. Damn, she looks good in it. So much so that I don't want to sell this boat in two days to the customer I have lined up.

"Aren't you going to come aboard?" Her voice has a flirtatious lilt, and I toe out of my shoes and hop on board.

I put the key in the ignition while her eyes take in everything. "Sadly, no sex on the boat. Everyone would see us."

She laughs. "We could dock somewhere."

"We could, but it's dusk, and these old boats don't have lights like our fishing ones."

"Don't worry, I have a place for us that's not too far away after the ride."

I get us out of the marina to the open water, and Chevelle pulls her hair into a ponytail once the wind hits us. She snuggles up to my side and lays her head on my shoulder.

Just a few years ago, I never would've thought this was something I wanted—to be responsible for someone besides myself. I'm not financially responsible for Chevelle. She does that all by herself, but her happiness is in my hands to a certain extent. And instead of that scaring me, I'm glad I'm the one who gets her to smile every day.

I slow the boat once we get to a spot I took a lot of my charters to fish, and we coast. Her hand moves to my thigh.

"Remember, I said no sex," I say.

She giggles. "You're not really going to make me have a sex-off with you, are you?"

"Sex-off?"

"See which one of us can go the longest without sex."

I turn to face her. "You assume you'd win?"

She laughs. "I know I'd win."

"You make it tempting to beat you, but I'm gonna throw in the white towel. I haven't had you in half of the positions I want you in. Maybe we can play that game after a few kids." I chuckle and tip her head back, placing my lips on hers.

"Thank goodness. I thought I talked myself into a corner there."

I run my hands over the wheel, still in awe at the course my life is headed. That I had the guts to stand up to my dad.

"Thank you." My voice is soft, and she looks at me, tilting her head. I kiss her again and draw back. "Thank you for believing in me."

She smiles, and damn, I wish we weren't on the boat right now. "You were already making the boats. You sold two before I ever even knew about it."

"Yeah, but to stand up to my father... to leave the family business and the security I had there... I never would've done that without you. I always thought it's what made me worthwhile, you know?"

She shakes her head. "I wish you saw yourself like I did."

"Tell me again about how you crushed on me?" I wink and she shakes her head with a laugh. "I want to know a time you were into me and trying to hide it."

She looks up, thinking for a minute, then looks back at me. "Hawaii. When we went out to the club. I would've slept with you that night."

Damn. "Are you serious? I tried to be a gentleman."

She laughs. "Didn't you wonder why I was grinding into

you on the dance floor? Or how I chose your room to escape from the grandmas? I could've slept with Mandi in her bed."

None of that ever crossed my mind. "You mean I could've had you over a year ago?"

I lean in closer and kiss her again, but this time she wraps her arms around my neck and draws me deeper. I lose all track of our surroundings and the fact I didn't anchor the boat until a horn sounds and I see a fishing boat coming right toward us. I start the engine and get us out of harm's way.

"You're a distraction," I say.

She doesn't respond but lets the wind hit her face. She's so beautiful, and I can't believe she's mine.

"Want to drive?" I ask her a few minutes later.

"Are you sure?"

"We'll have one of our own one day. Might as well get used to it." I turn into an alcove, and we make the switch. She looks even better behind the wheel.

"Thanks." She hammers on the gas, and I shake my head as she really sees what this boat can do.

AFTER WE LEAVE the boat at the Winterberry Falls Marina in the slip I rented a few days ago, I drive us up the mountain until we're at a lookout point. I leave her blindfolded in the jeep while I set out those fake lights that resemble candlelight. I don't want to burn down the woods because we get too far into ourselves.

"I like the blindfold in bed much better," she says.

I remove it from her eyes and her mouth opens into an O.

"I'll remember that." I chuckle.

I bring her over to the picnic I made for us with the fake candles. I have blankets to keep us warm. The small cliff overlooks the lake, and because it's dusk, you can see the fishing boats coming in and out.

"Could you ever imagine being a fisherwoman on one of the big boats that stay out at sea for weeks at a time?" I ask, pouring her a glass of white wine.

"I considered it, but I'm not sure I could live on a boat with all men. I wish there were more women in the field. Also, my family..." She sips her wine.

"Being away from them?"

She nods. "After..." Her eyes find mine over the rim of her glass. "I just never wanted to be far away from them."

I don't say anything, hoping she continues. I'm desperate for her to open up to me about losing her mom and the pain it's caused because I want to help her heal. I know that's a superhuman expectation, but she's been through enough in this lifetime.

"I never want to miss a moment. Just in case."

I don't give her a look of pity because that's a sure way of getting her to stop talking.

"I think a lot of people wish they'd do that. There are a lot of memories I think I've forgotten over the years." Which is the truth.

"There are some I don't think I'll ever forget. But being the youngest, I remember Mom the least. I used to be jealous of Cade, because he could recall everything about our mom because he's the oldest. All I have is the way she hugged me when she reached me on the ice. The pat of her hand on my back, ushering me toward my dad. I feel like after she died, that's the only memory that stuck in my head. As if it erased all others." She sets down the wine and stares at the darkening sky. "Then I hear my dad's screams, see his face transforming in horror. Him lunging forward and my brothers grabbing me."

No tears fall from her eyes. I'm sure she's recounted this moment so many times that she can do it on autopilot.

She looks at me. "I'm ruining our night. I'm sorry."

I take her hands and scoot closer to her. "Never be sorry. I want you to trust me. I want you to open up to me so I can help you heal."

She tilts her head and stares at me for a moment with a sad smile. "I'm not sure I'll ever heal. I think this is just the way it is. I came to the realization a long time ago, after years of therapy, that I'll just live my life feeling guilty about what happened."

"You were five." I brush my thumb down her cheek.

"At five, you should know not to go on the ice. Especially when you live in Alaska. It was so stupid of me." She hangs her head low.

"Have you thought about going back to therapy?" I refuse to let her live the rest of her life taking the blame for her mom's death when she was so young.

"I went for years, and I'm sure it got me to where I am now. Functional, able to laugh, able to have fun." She looks more intently at me. "I'm not sitting at home crying every night, you know that."

Maybe I am trying to be superhuman and fix it all for her. When something so tragic happens, maybe it just hangs there above people like a rain cloud and sometimes it pours. I loved Mrs. Greene like a mother, and I used to hear Fisher cry sometimes when I'd spend the night. Something out of the blue would set him off and he'd retreat, no longer wanting to play or do whatever we were doing. Time seemed to heal those wounds for him.

"After it happened, I remember you were a shell sometimes," I say. "Just sat at the end of the table and ate your dinner. Then you'd go to your room. I always had this pull toward you, wanting to help you, even as kids—ever since I saw you on the swings at your mom's wake."

She smiles at me. "I remember that. You got me to eat, then I climbed the trellis and told you not to look up my dress."

"Your dad never took it down."

"Because we moved to the big house. I'm sure Fisher will before Laurie is a teenager."

We both laugh. I think that instead of trying to heal that wound that might never scar over, maybe I just need to fill her life with love and laughter. Not dwell in the past.

"Tell me how many kids you want?" I ask, changing the subject.

She pushes my shoulder. "What kind of question is that?"

"We have to make sure we're compatible. How many kids?" She looks at me for a long beat and I slide closer, tucking a strand of her hair behind her ear. "I'm in this for the long haul, Chevelle. I want you to know that." She says nothing, and I know thinking of the future scares her, but I need to try to nudge her in that direction from time to time. "I want at least two. No only child, because it sucks. After that, I'll leave it up to you. It's your body."

"Oh, how sweet of you." She rolls her eyes.

I kiss her and get her on her back. "Let's get started now."

I'm joking, of course, but I think she's relieved to be done with all our deep thoughts. I pull out a condom ten minutes later, after we're naked and unable to stop ourselves from having sex in public.

Everything about her fits. We're perfect together.

Chapter Twenty-four

Chevelle

I slide under the sheet next to Cam. We've had sex every night, whether it's while we're watching a movie and his hand slides under the blanket and up my thigh or when we go to bed. He's insatiable, and he's made me insatiable. But he's given me the gift of oral sex a lot more than I have him, so since I woke up early today, I figure I'll surprise him.

He's grown accustomed to sleeping naked as well, so I don't have to fiddle with boxers or shorts. He's already half chub when my hand lightly handles him under the sheet. He must be having a great dream.

I pump him a few times. No movement from him. Then I put my mouth on him, my tongue swirling around his tip before I lower my mouth and take in his entire length. His dick grows in my mouth, and a moan slips from him above the sheets.

"You should know I have a girlfriend," he says and laughs. He tears the sheets off of me. "And I like to watch."

I give him my best bored look, but it's too hard with his dick in my mouth. As annoying as I used to find him, he makes me laugh all the time.

He rests his hands behind his head. "Carry on."

"Be careful, dear, or I'll use my teeth."

He scrunches away, and his hands fly down to cover his dick. "That's not even a joke. What if I told you I was going to shove a... I don't know, I can't think, you got me all hot with that succulent mouth of yours."

I laugh. "Here's a tip. When your girlfriend goes down on you, you enjoy it and don't talk."

The smile falls from his face, and he stares at me.

"What?" I ask, running what I said through my mind.

"Say it again." He touches my cheek, his thumb running along my bottom lip.

"Be quiet when I'm sucking you and enjoy it?"

He shakes his head, then it dawns on me.

"The girlfriend part?"

He nods and smiles.

"Oh." I get up on my knees between his legs. "Sorry, are we not there yet? I thought since you'd just used the word and since we weren't—"

"Of course we're fucking there. I love that you referred to yourself as my girlfriend. I haven't heard you say it yet."

I feel my cheeks heat. "Well yeah, I'm not seeing anyone else, and..."

He sits up and plasters his hands to my cheeks, kissing me until he has me on my back. His lips continue a path across my jaw and down my neck. "And we'll always remember that when you first referred to yourself as my girlfriend, your mouth was millimeters away from my cock."

"Cam!" I smack his arm.

"It's a good memory. Really." Then his body covers mine again.

"Don't you want a blow job?"

He's already reaching for the nightstand drawer where we keep the condoms. "Maybe when I ask you to marry me, we can do a replay. Right now, I just wanna be deep inside of you while you call me your boyfriend over and over again."

"Was it that much of a big deal?"

He sits up from kissing my breast. "Yes, a very big deal. We're progressing."

I shake my head and chuckle. "Whatever you say."

As the words leave my mouth, Cam studies me and sets the condom to the side, still in its wrapper. His lips cascade over my body like little butterfly touches, and even his hands brush and glide instead of grab and pull.

"You're so gorgeous. I don't deserve you," he murmurs along my skin.

At first, I'm not sure how to respond to the lethargic pace he's setting because he's not fucking me. He's making love. I've never made love with anyone.

He nibbles on my earlobe, his hot breath causing goose bumps to erupt along my neck. "My sweet girlfriend."

I can feel his smile on my skin. Making him so happy is a euphoric feeling. I run my hands down his strong back muscles, and his thigh moves my legs wider apart, making room for him. He rises up on his elbows and moves my hair out of the way. His eyes lock with mine and I decide I don't want anything between us. He reaches for the condom, but I find myself shaking my head.

"What?" he asks, kissing the corner of my mouth.

"I have an IUD and I'm clean."

He stares at me for a long time. "Me too." He shakes his head. "I mean clean. No IUD."

I laugh and lower my hands to his ass, pushing him so the tip of his dick enters me.

"Are you sure? I'm in no rush."

I nod. "I'm positive."

He bites his lip. "Well, shit, I feel like my manhood is about to be challenged."

My head rears back in laughter. "Why?" I ask once I regain control of myself.

"Because being inside you bare, it's going to be hard as hell not to come immediately. If I'm staring off into space, it's just because I'm thinking about that duck chasing me instead of your warm, wet pussy."

I shake my head. "Cam?"

He runs his finger along my hairline again. "Yes, girlfriend?"

"Get inside me."

"So bossy." He slides into me, and I open wider for him, making room for his hips. "Oh shit."

"Already?" I ask.

He smiles at me. "No."

He lowers his body and captures my lips as he circles his hips, making love to me, tattooing himself to my soul and lasting a lot longer than either of us thought he would.

If he thinks my referring to myself as his girlfriend is big, he'd probably fall over if I admitted the truth—I love him.

"You want us over for dinner?" I ask Marla for the fourth time since she called me after work today. "Why? It's Cam."

"Yes, it's Cam, and we want to meet him as your special someone."

Special someone? "Okay."

"Good. Dinner is on Sunday."

I grip the phone tighter. "Sunday? That's family dinner night."

"Yes," she says. "His role in our family has changed now."

"You can't be serious."

"Be here by five. No need to bring anything. I've got it all handled. Gotta go. See you then." She hangs up before I can argue with her. Damn that woman.

I arrive home a few minutes later and Cam is on the floor of the family room with Gunner up on the couch. He's sketching a new design for an older boat he just bought.

"Hey, girlfriend," he says because he can't seem to stop referring to me by that moniker.

"Hey, boyfriend." I walk over, and Gunner gets up, coming over to me so I'll pet him, which I do. "We've been summoned to the big house."

His pencil drops. "Really?"

I nod. "Sunday dinner."

"Shit." He cringes even though we know my family already thinks of him as one of us. "Am I going to be drilled with questions?"

I sit on the sofa behind him, so his back is between my legs. I massage his shoulders.

He lays his head on my thigh. "I'll make you proud, girl-friend. I promise."

"You can stop calling me girlfriend." I squeeze a little harder to get my point across.

"Why, girlfriend?"

I stop massaging, holding up my hands.

"Okay, girlfriend. I'll stop." I move to get up, but he stops me, turning around and somehow getting me on my back. "I'll stop now. For the rest of the night."

"Uh-huh."

He does stop for ten minutes while we have sex on the couch. But after that, he's back to calling me girlfriend practically every other word. It's somewhat annoying, but there are worse things, right?

SUNDAY COMES WAY TOO QUICKLY, and Cam disappeared this morning only to return with a bouquet of flowers for Marla and my dad's favorite barbeque sauce from a store in Greywall.

"Why did you buy this stuff?" I ask as we walk up the hill toward the house, where most of my siblings' cars are already parked. I had my suspicions but hoped it would just be the four of us.

"I'm coming as your boyfriend tonight." I stare at him, and he holds up his hands. "I didn't call you girlfriend." He lowers his head to mine. "Girlfriend."

I swat at his arm, and he laughs.

"Seriously, I'm not coming as Fisher's best friend. I'm coming as your guy."

"I like that my guy thing." I step closer and tilt my head toward him. He doesn't miss the fact I'm looking for another kiss and places his lips on mine. "I apologize ahead of time for their behavior. I know they're going to do something bizarre or embarrassing, so just roll with it."

He literally vacations with us and has been part of our family forever. I'm not sure why I'm so worried my family is going to embarrass me. Ha! Yes, I do. It's because I know them.

I walk in through the garage and the house is eerily quiet when I know there are at least five babies here.

"We're here," I announce. "You know, just me and Cam, the guy you've known forever."

We round the corner, and sure enough, my family is all sitting there and staring at us.

Marla gets up from the couch. "Hello, Chevelle and…" She looks at Cam, apparently waiting for me to introduce him.

I scrunch my eyebrows. "Cam."

"Cam? Does Cam have a last name?" she asks like she's never met him before.

"Baker," I say slowly, not understanding why they're pretending we don't know him.

She holds out her hand. "Nice to meet you, Cam Baker. May I assume Cam is short for Cameron?"

"You may." Cam shakes her hand and looks at me.

I shrug and shake my head. Like, just go with it, I guess.

"I brought you some flowers," he says.

Marla accepts them and turns to the group. "He brought flowers. And they smell great. I'll go put these in water. Why don't you introduce Cam to the rest of the family?" She walks into the kitchen.

Now all my siblings are looking at us with serious faces. We step farther into the family room.

"This is Cameron Baker, everyone, but you already know that." I turn to my dad. "This is my dad, Hank."

Cam hands him the bottle of barbeque sauce, and my dad lifts it to look at it. "My favorite. Thank you."

"You're welcome."

Cade is next to my dad, and he puts out his hand. "I'm Cade, Chevelle's oldest brother. This is my wife, Presley, and our little girl, Morgan. Our daughter, Leighton, is downstairs with our brother, Rylan."

Cam goes along with it all and shakes hands. We make our way through the room, and I do introductions with everyone until we reach Fisher.

"This is so stupid," I mumble.

Fisher stares at Cam's hand.

"Fisher, this is your best friend, Cam. And now he's also my boyfriend." I do the introduction as Allie bites her lip to keep from laughing. "And this is his wife, Allie. They have a set of twins, Axel and Laurie, who I assume are with Rylan in the basement."

Cam puts his hand out, and Fisher shakes it. I'm not sure how much the two have talked since Fisher found us at his place, but they seem to be having some nonverbal conversation with their handshake and nods.

Marla comes back into the living room. "Everyone get introduced?"

"Yes, and this is weird, even for us." I look around the room for one of my siblings to agree with me, but no one says anything.

"Then it's settled." Marla puts her hand on my dad's shoulder and looks at Cam.

"What?" My forehead wrinkles.

"Welcome to the family, Cam. We couldn't be happier that Chevelle picked you." Marla hugs him.

Everyone else in the family swarms him with a big welcome. Once Cam is out from the middle of everyone, he pulls me into his side.

"This was cheesy," I say. "At least I don't have to be embarrassed because you were already a member of this family."

Cam kisses me, and the room grows quiet.

"Okay, that's just weird," Fisher says. "I vote no PDA in front of the family."

"Well, get used to it." I fist Cam's shirt and pull him to me again, giving him a big kiss.

The collective groans from my brothers make me chuckle against Cam's lips.

My family is so odd, but they're all mine.

Chapter Twenty-five

Cam

I'm at the warehouse, working on the new boat, when my cell phone rings. My dad's name flashes across the screen.

"Hello?"

"Cam, it's Dad." As if I didn't know.

"Hey."

"I was wondering if I could come by and talk to you."

"Come by where?" Usually he's summoning me to his perch at the marina.

"Wherever you want to meet."

The last place I want him to be is here. He'll probably judge the space. I can only imagine the list of things he would say I need to change.

"Okay, how about a restaurant? When?" I ask.

"The sooner, the better."

"Well, I'm at the warehouse for Five Seas right now, but I can get back into town in a bit."

"Do you mind if I come to you?"

What the hell is going on with him?

"There's a restaurant attached to the marina. It's casual. We can meet there." I am not letting him into this warehouse.

"Okay, I'll be there in an hour for lunch." He hangs up.

For some reason, I feel uncomfortable about this meeting. It's as if my intuition knows something is coming, and I might not like it.

I text Chevelle even though I'm sure she's out on a charter.

> My dad just called and wants to meet with me right away.

No response, which I expected. She's busy working.

> I can't imagine what he wants.

I set my phone on the table, now unable to concentrate on what I was doing before my dad called. For the next hour, I don't get any work done. I start just to stop and worry if he has something he'll try to use over me to get me back in the family business. My dad didn't get to where he is without being a little underhanded.

I'm actually thankful when it's time to meet him, just so I can get whatever this is over with.

The restaurant is a hole-in-the-wall place that serves great fish, fries and hushpuppies. Not my dad's style, but then again, he did ask to come my way.

My phone rings right when my hand meets the door. I relax when I see it's Chevelle.

"Hey," I answer.

"I'm so glad I caught you. No matter what he wants, remember you're doing what you love. Don't let him steer you away from that, okay?"

I smile at how much she sounds like a motivational coach. "I know, and I won't."

"Maybe we're overthinking this. Maybe he wants to mend fences."

"Yeah, right."

She's silent. Probably because she knows as well as I do that the probability of that is slim. "Call me as soon as you finish. I have a break for an hour before a four-hour charter, but I could sneak a few texts if you need me."

"Thanks."

"Cam, you've got this."

I nod although she can't see me. "Thank you."

"You're welcome."

We hang up as I see my dad park his Range Rover in the lot. Figuring I want to have the pick of where we sit, I walk into the restaurant and take a table by the window. I sit with my back to the wall, so I'm prepared for anything.

The waitress, Bella, greets me first. "Hey, Cam."

Since I come here three times a week now, most people in the marina know who I am and what I do.

"Hi, Bella, just a Coke and..." I signal to my dad, who's crossing the room.

He takes off his suit jacket and puts it on the back of the chair.

"Can I get you something?" Bella asks him.

My dad looks at where the menu is posted on the wall. "Just an ice water actually."

"I'll be right back." Bella's braids bounce as she goes to get our drinks.

He looks around and out at the marina. "This is a nice place. Not as many slips as we have, but..."

"Yeah, it's smaller. They don't get the fishing boats we do. But they had room, and I didn't want to be in Sunrise Bay."

"That was a question I wanted to ask you the day you told me about all this. Why were you so worried? I've seen those boats, Cameron. They're exceptional."

I shrug.

He sighs and steeples his hands. "Listen, your mother and I had a long conversation the other night. She made me realize that maybe I've been too hard on you."

I open my mouth to speak, but Bella comes over with our drinks. We both order the daily special of fish, fries and hushpuppies.

"Dad, I—"

"No, please let me finish. This is important." He pauses. "The marina has been in our family a long time. I was different than you. I was eager to run the marina. My dad was hard on me like I am on you, and I followed in his footsteps because I thought that's what you do. The more you rebelled, the harder I pressed you."

I don't say anything but sip my drink. Hearing my dad talk about something he thinks he should have done differently is surreal—it almost never happens.

"I never bothered to ask you what you wanted, and when you disappointed me, I felt like you were disrespecting me, oftentimes on purpose. A lot of times, it felt like the whole town knew you'd rather be with the Greene family than your own. That hurt me. But instead of talking to you about it, I was angry. If you love building wooden boats, then okay, you should do that."

He looks out the window a little wistfully, and I get the feeling it's because he can't handle looking at me after being so open and vulnerable.

"I never meant to disrespect you. I thought I wanted to run the marina too. I never saw myself doing anything different. Until it wasn't fun anymore. Until I saw how some of the decisions we'd make would affect people. I don't like the business side of it, Dad. The one where we have to kick people out or watch families suffer while we take such a huge cut of their catch. Restoring and selling boats... it's not the same. I still need the education you gave me, but I don't have to worry about hurting anyone when I'm just selling a luxury item."

He sighs. "You think I enjoy that? It's the worst part of the job. But it's part of business, and it has to be done."

"It's the part I hate."

"Well, clearly, if you stayed in the position, you'd bankrupt the marina." He smiles, so I know he's saying it in jest. "Paying their slip fees for them isn't helping. Not long term." He gives me a hard glare.

Guess he figured out about Rowdy's bill.

He laughs. I'm not sure the last time I heard my dad laugh. "When I saw that, I was proud and pissed all at the same time."

"You should also know that the reason I didn't want to start the fishing charter business is because it would compete with Chevelle."

His head rocks back. "That's my second reason for coming here. I see you two around."

"We're together now."

"I know." He nods.

Bella brings our meals and sets them in front of us. I dig in right away.

"That's another area I should've listened to you. I'm sorry, Cam."

"It's okay. It ended up not really affecting her business. Those two boats are for different kinds of people and budgets."

He nods. "I went a little crazy when I ordered it."

We eat our meals quietly for a bit. I'm not sure where our relationship goes from here.

"Your mom would like to have you and Chevelle over for dinner."

"I'm sure Chevelle would like that. Just let us know when."

He nods and splits apart his fried fish. Then he drops both pieces, wipes his hands, and looks at me. My body tenses over what he might say.

"I'm proud of you, Cam. You did what not many have the guts to do. You put yourself out there, not knowing what the outcome would be. I have no doubt Five Seas will be a great success." He picks up his water, and we clink our plastic glasses. "Now, where do I order one? I can get to the front of the list since I'm your father, right?" He smiles.

I can't help but grin back. "I'll see what I can do."

After lunch, my dad shakes my hand and pulls me in for a hug. "We need to do this again. That was the best fish I've ever eaten."

I nod. "Okay."

Feeling a little lighter, I watch him walk back to his Range Rover. Maybe now that I don't have to have a business relationship with my dad, we can learn to be father and son. I text Chevelle, asking her to call me when she has an opportunity.

My phone rings in my pocket as I walk back to the warehouse. "Hey."

"I'm just about to board my boat. Good meeting or bad meeting?" she asks.

"My mom wants us over for dinner, and he wants to order a boat from me." I'm still speechless.

"So good meeting!"

"Yeah, definitely a good meeting."

"Oh, that's great, Cam."

I'll need more than one meeting to be confident he's really changed, but I can't help but feel hopeful. "Yeah, it is. Now go on your charter and I'll see you at home tonight."

"We're going to celebrate! Bye, boyfriend."

I laugh. "See you, girlfriend."

We hang up as I get to the warehouse, finally able to concentrate on getting the next boat finished.

Who am I kidding? I just daydream about going home to Chevelle. I'm one lucky bastard.

Chapter Twenty-six

Chevelle

Two weeks later, I'm getting ready for one of my last fishing excursions of the season. I plan on using my off time to help Cam with his new business.

But right now, he's helping me with mine. We're currently walking down the dock toward my boat.

"Now, remember," I say. "You are here as an *employee*."

"I don't recall you mentioning that I'd be paid." He looks at me and winks.

"I pay you plenty."

He laughs. "I think I pay you back in kind."

"Very true. But seriously, you are not the boss of this charter. I am the boss."

I asked Cam to come with me for two reasons, the first being that I want to spend time with him. Second, being that he was a little forceful with his constant asking if he could come along. I'm finding it easier to ask him for help, so I asked him to join. This charter is three hours with six men, and as much as I hate to admit it, I could use an extra hand.

He holds up both hands. "I'm just your measly employee. Low man on the ladder. I get it."

"Well, you could think of some things the boss might like to win her over."

He grabs me by my waist and pulls me toward him. "Say the word and I'll strip you down right here."

"You wouldn't."

"You're right, I wouldn't." He smacks a kiss on my lips and releases me. Sadly.

We climb aboard my boat, and he helps me prepare for the charter. He puts the poles in the holding tubes while I prepare the beer and snacks.

"I kind of like this working as a team," I say once we're ready to go.

And perfect timing, because our charter guests are walking up the dock. I step out of the boat to greet them. All six of them are probably in their forties, rings gleaming on their left ring fingers. Hopefully all they want to do is fish, not party.

I welcome the group, and they all climb on board. I introduce Cam and go over the safety guidelines. They listen attentively, and I pull out of the marina into open waters ten minutes later.

Cam chats with the guys as I'm getting us to the fishing spot we decided on. These men have more experience than I usually get in charters, so I want to make them happy so they'll return next year.

They cast their lures, and I put out refreshments on the table and ask them if they want a beer. Some take me up on it and others don't. It's one of the easiest charters I've had this year.

Cam sits with me in the wheelhouse so they can do their own thing. "I'm not liking these clouds. What did radar say when you checked it?"

I look in the direction he's pointing, but I checked as I always do, and our route was fine. There was a storm that would hit northwest of us, but we were clear.

"It's all clear by us." I pull out my phone and hand it to him.

He zooms in and out, moving the screen up and down. "Looks like it. Those dark clouds look like they're heading right this way. But I'm not a weatherman." He shrugs.

I tilt my head back, resting my neck on the chair, and stare at the sky. We still have two hours left, and I hope the weather holds off so this group can have a memorable excursion that they'll want to relive next year.

The spot we're in ends up being a bust, so Cam suggests a different spot and the guys are all up for it. We'll need to go slightly northwest, but we both look at the radar again and it still says the storm will miss us.

Once we get to the new spot, everyone sets out their poles again. Cam comes over when the guys are chatting. Supposedly, four of them live in Alaska and two of them have moved down to the lower forty-eight. Which explains why some of them look familiar to me.

"What do you want to do after this?" Cam asks, lifting my legs and putting them across his. Very unprofessional, but the men are engaged in their conversation about their college years.

He massages my calves. It feels good after being on my feet so much, squeezing in every last charter before I have to shut down for the season.

"I just want to grab some food and chill."

"You do realize we're turning into an old couple, right? And we don't even have kids."

I raise my eyebrows.

"We could change that if you want?"

"Go to a bar?" I groan just thinking about it.

"No, have kids."

"Cam, we've been together a few weeks. You're insane."

He laughs as a few raindrops land on my arms. I look at my windshield, and sure enough, there is more.

"Let me see your phone again," Cam says, and I hand it to him.

He checks the weather, zooming in and out on the screen before he looks at me. I know the minute he does what he's going to say. "We gotta go."

He's not asking my permission or even making it a suggestion. It's an order, which makes me grind my teeth. He walks to the back by the guys and tells them all to pack up because a storm is going to hit right over us and he can't tell how bad it might get.

As experienced as they are, they don't question him but pull their poles out of the water and put everything away.

"I'm sorry, guys," I say.

"That's the thing about fishing. Weather's always an issue." The one guy smiles.

I lift the anchor as they finish getting everything together and the rain comes down harder.

What a way to end the last charter of my season. I'm so annoyed.

I hear Rowdy calling me over the sound of the rain on the water. "Chevelle. Over."

"Go ahead, Rowdy. It's Cam. Over." He snatches the radio from my hand as I scowl at him.

The men are putting on rain jackets, that's how prepared they are.

"Cam. The storm turned direction at the last minute. You either find a place to hunker down or get back. Over."

"We're coming back. Over." Cam's gaze darts to me.

"Then hurry. Over."

Cam puts the radio back and tries to take the wheel.

"Excuse me." I stay where I am.

"Chevelle." He eyes me.

The guys are staring at us, probably wondering why we're having a standoff in the middle of a rainstorm.

"I'm the one in charge. You're the employee. Remember?"

He sighs but lifts his hands. "Fine."

While he sits behind me, I maneuver us toward the marina. Rain pelts down on us as the sky grows darker. My lights barely make our route visible with the sheets of rain coming down. Water coats the windshield in front of me and I instinctively squint, as if that will help me see better. We're close to the marina. I see the lights, but a boom of thunder hits, so loud I'd think it was right next to us.

"Everyone okay?" I shout and take a quick look behind me.

They all nod.

I let up on the speed a bit to see where I'm going. The last thing I want is to crash into the dock.

Cam comes up behind me. "Don't slow down, keep going. You slow and—"

The boat tips over a big wave, but I adjust our position and recover.

He stands beside me. "It's gonna be tricky coming into the marina against the wind until we've passed the breakers."

"I know. I've been doing this longer than you." Which isn't necessarily true. Cam has probably been on the water most of his life. And the truth is, I've never been in weather this bad.

"You need to accelerate, Chevelle. The boat will never—"

We tip again, and I correct us.

"*Cliff!*" a man screams, and I turn, spotting a body in orange floating by the boat.

"Shit." I slow the boat and turn around to get him.

"Goddamn it." Cam dives into the water.

"*No!*" I yell. "*Cam!*"

The men are all watching but staying in their seats, eyes wide. Thank God, because men who aren't fishermen would've gone to the side their friend went over and we'd have capsized by now.

Cam reaches Cliff, but Cliff panics and pushes Cam under the water. Cam's arms flail, and he pops up only for a panicked Cliff to press him down again.

"*No!*" I look at the guys. "One of you take over."

I jump in, swimming over to them. I pry Cliff's hands off Cam, but Cliff hangs on to me, using me as his buoy. I should've put them in vests when the storm started. As if the guys on the boat can read my mind, they throw some our way.

Cliff presses on my shoulders again, and I sink, choking on water. A mouthful of saltwater makes me gag, and I feel someone pull me up to the surface.

Cam holds me at his side. "Take him." He's pushing Cliff, who has blood dripping from his nose, toward my boat.

Rowdy's there now with his boat, shining his light on us. Gage is in the boat as well. "You guys okay?" he shouts over the storm.

The guys grab Cliff and pull him into my boat.

"Gage, you go in Chevelle's boat, get them back to the marina. Rowdy, we're coming with you. Someone call the paramedics." Cam is dictating as I continue to cough up saltwater.

Rowdy helps us into his boat as we watch Gage drive my

boat into the marina as though someone is dying. I guess that's what Cam wanted me to do.

Once we're in Rowdy's boat, Rowdy throws some blankets over us. "You gotta get out of those clothes."

"Just get us out of here," Cam says and doesn't even use a blanket. He's too worried about me. He rubs his hands on my arms, lowering to my eye level. "Are you okay?" He inspects my body.

"You shouldn't have dived in!" I shout.

"You shouldn't have dived in. I had it under control."

"He was drowning you."

"I had it under control, Chevelle."

The paramedics arrive at the marina shortly after we dock. Turns out Cam broke Cliff's nose trying to get him off of me since Cliff was panicked and going to drown one of us to save his own life.

When we get home, Cam draws me a bath, and the lukewarm water helps bring my body temp back up to where it needs to be. As I sink under the bathwater, the reality of what just happened hits me like a Mack truck. I almost killed another person I love.

"Talk to me," Cam says, climbing in with me once I come up for air.

"I almost killed you," I say. "I was too stubborn to let you drive. I was hell-bent on proving I could do it, and I almost lost you like—" I don't even want to think about what it would feel like to be sitting here alone without his strong arms around me.

He kisses my temple and tightens his hold. "I'm here. I'm right here."

I nod, but we're just lucky things went our way. All I can think of right now is what if. What if they hadn't?

Cam

It's been a week since her charter, and every day, I feel Chevelle pull a little farther away. I've tried everything to get her to see reality, but she believes the whole incident was her fault. So, I'm going to the only person I think might be able to help me.

I knock on his door, thankful he called reinforcements.

Allie opens the door. "Hey, Cam."

Hank sits on the couch, playing peekaboo with Axel between his legs. "Cam," he says with a nod.

Fisher runs down the stairs, freshly showered and putting on a shirt. "Hey, man."

He fist-bumps me but then encases me in a hug. I've seen Fisher already since the accident, but everyone keeps hugging me as though I was near death. But I know where it's coming from. I've lived in this town my whole life, and we've all seen tragic nights like that one. That's why I don't blame Chevelle. The open water is a wicked mistress, and she does what she wants when she wants.

"Have a seat. Axel and Laurie are going to enjoy their new basement." Allie acts excited, and the two little ones run over to the basement door.

"Thanks, babe." Fisher sits on the couch, and Allie nods at him.

I take a seat next to Fisher and don't say anything at first, trying to figure out where to start, but Hank saves me the trouble.

"So..." he says. "She's drowning in guilt?"

I nod. "I've tried everything. Nothing works. Every day I feel her pulling farther away. I tried to get her out on my dad's boat just for a ride on the water, and she said no."

Hank frowns. "We all know she's never been ice-skating or even come close to a frozen pond since Laurie's accident." He blows out a breath. "I'd hate for her to lose her livelihood because of a near miss. When I was sick last year, at first she refused to even talk to me about it, and then when she did, she acted like she was gonna be my savior."

We sit quietly for a second, each of us in our thoughts.

"I could give her more time, but I don't think that's the answer," I confess.

"What about therapy?" Fisher says, picking up from beside the couch that old safe that he had a couple weeks ago and examining it again as though it will just spring open in his hands.

"Still can't get that thing open?" I ask.

Fisher shakes his head.

Hank looks at it and stills. "Where did you find that?"

Fisher gives me a mischievous grin. Just like he used to when Hank caught us doing something we shouldn't and got us in trouble. "The basement."

"Let me see it." Hank holds out his hands and takes it, giving it a good once-over. "This was your mother's."

"Yeah?" Fisher's eyebrows rise into his hairline.

"Where in the basement?"

"It was behind a cinder block, way back in the crawl space."

Hank huffs and tries the lock.

"So you recognize it?" Fisher asks.

He nods. "Your mother put it together. There are things inside... I'm not sure what. She wouldn't tell me." He looks at it longingly. "I completely forgot about this."

"What was it for?" Fisher asks.

"Two years before she died, she felt a lump in her breast." He continues to study the safe as if he's remembering little by little. "Your mom convinced herself she had cancer and asked me to get her one of these small safes. She didn't want any of you kids to be able to get into it. I obliged because I loved her, but I kept saying we should just wait until she'd gone in for the ultrasound. Whatever is in here" —he jiggles it—"she put in there because she thought she was dying."

"Why would she do that and not give you the key?" Fisher asks.

"I think she did. Maybe. I don't know. Why didn't she destroy it after we found out it was just a fatty deposit? Why keep it?"

Answers they'll never get since Mrs. Greene died.

"My assumption is she forgot about it too." Hank hands it back to Fisher. "Raising five kids... we were busy, and it probably slipped her mind. I guess the question is, do you want to open it?"

Fisher sighs and looks at it. "I don't know. I guess it needs to be a joint sibling decision, right? I don't want to open Pandora's box, and them all hate me for whatever's in here."

Hank chuckles. "I think your siblings would be happy to have anything that was your mother's. But you're right. It's a sibling decision." He eyes Fisher. "Maybe we can kill two birds with one stone—help your sister and see what's in that thing."

Fisher glances at me then down at the safe. He nods and turns to me, and I know what his plan is. "I'm sorry, man, you can't be part of this one. It's a sibling thing, but if it works, she's gonna be okay."

I nod, trusting my best friend.

Hank smiles at his son. Everyone knows Fisher isn't a sentimental guy, so what he's about to do, opening this thing up in front of his siblings when no one knows what's inside, is a big deal.

"Thank you." I stand.

"Don't thank me until it works."

I leave Fisher's and head back to our house, hoping Chevelle is ready to face this fear and tackle it once and for all.

When I get home, Chevelle is on the couch, Gunner snuggled in next to her. They're watching television.

Obviously, Fisher hasn't called yet.

"Want to come to the warehouse with me? You were supposed to be my partner this off-season." I sit in the chair adjacent to her.

She shakes her head. "I'm about to find out who the father is."

I pick up the remote and click off the TV.

"Cam!" she shouts.

I slide onto the coffee table in front of her. "Listen, Chevelle, I know you're shaken. I'm shaken. It was scary, but we're both still here. Still living. Except you're not living, you're hiding."

"You don't understand."

"I do!" I shout. Realizing that won't solve anything, I lower my voice. "I do understand. I was there. I know how scared I was when I saw Cliff push you under the water. You think I'm not scared shitless that I almost lost you? You think I won't worry every time you're out on the water without me? And I wish, oh how I wish I could promise you that nothing will ever happen to me. That you'll never lose me. But then I'd break that promise at some point and I don't break promises to you."

Tears fall from her eyes. She quickly wipes them away.

I slide to the end of the table, reaching for her. She sits up and Gunner places his head on her lap, staring up at her. "I don't break my word to you. Ever. But what happened is no reason to stop living. If you're not busy living, you're busy dying."

Her phone rings on the table, but she doesn't reach for it.

I grab it when I see Fisher's name on the screen and hand it to her. "I think you should answer this."

She looks at the phone and scrunches her eyes. Clearing her throat, she accepts the call, "Hey. Fish... uh-huh... no... why... Fine... okay." She hangs up.

Clearly, it took some pushing on Fisher's part.

"Are you in on this?" she asks, sounding put out.

"On what?"

"The fact that we're all going to my mom's grave? It's like payback because I've done it to two people I lo... never mind."

I bite the inside of my cheek, trying to not smile because she almost said love. "No."

She stands. "I'll go, but I don't understand why no one

can just give me some time." She continues to complain as she goes upstairs to change.

I pet Gunner. "Cross your paws, buddy. If this works, we'll get our happy, call-you-out-on-your-shit Chevelle back."

Chevelle

I arrive at Mom's gravesite. My brothers and my dad are already there, standing around waiting for me. I do not like being in this role. I like being the one who calls these meetings.

"Hello," I say with zero enthusiasm.

"Hey, Chevelle." Adam hugs me.

Then each of my brothers hugs me too. They're not normally that affectionate with me. Here we go again with them treating me like damaged goods. But I don't say anything. Instead, I take my place at the end of the line they've formed in front of Mom's grave.

"X?" Cade says, putting Xavier on FaceTime and passing his phone to my dad.

Usually when we're here, we each take turns talking to Mom, and I call out to the brother who can't get his head on straight. My dad sits on a bench nearby, holding the phone with Xavier's face on the screen. I read my mom's gravestone for the millionth time, sighing when I read how young she was when she died.

Fisher takes a small safe out of his duffel bag and puts it on her gravestone. "I found this in the basement."

"What is it?" Adam asks.

"It was Mom's," Fisher says.

They all look at me, and I roll my eyes.

"What? And you just found it now?" Cade looks at our dad.

"As I explained to Fisher, whatever's inside, your mom put it in there when she had a health scare about two years before she passed. Obviously everything turned out okay with her health, but when she put that safe together, she was convinced she was sick."

"Dad says we all have to agree on whether we want to open it or not." Fisher looks at us one by one.

"This seems unfair since I'm in San Francisco," Xavier says. "I could have flown… no, I couldn't." He pushes his hand through his hair and sighs. "My vote is to open it. If there's something in there specific to me, just keep it until I come home."

All eyes go to Cade. "I say we open it."

"Adam?" Fisher asks.

He nods. "Open."

"Open," Fisher says for his vote.

Again, they all look at me.

I'm scared to see what's inside, but I'm not the kind of person who can walk away without knowing. "We should open it."

Fisher picks it up, and my dad pulls a drill out of the bag sitting next to him.

"Okay then. You all agree. But before we open this, I want to say something." My dad holds the phone out to Cade, who takes it and turns it so Xavier's looking at our dad as he hands the drill to Fisher.

"Go ahead, Dad," Adam says.

"Your mom loved you all. You were her life. During this health scare, she was so worried about dying. Worried about leaving you all and not seeing you grow old. The relief when we found out it was nothing to worry about was one of the happiest days of our lives. And then the accident happened a couple of years later. She got two years more than she thought she'd have with you."

I lower my head. She could've had our entire lives.

"I feel like we need to talk this through as a family. We've dodged this conversation for years, and it's about time we put it to rest, here and now. Chevelle!" my dad barks.

I look up.

"She would've had it no other way. You were only five and just wanted to be with your brothers. As you will find out someday if you become a parent, you would give up your life for your child at any cost."

I look away, ashamed, but spot Cade, Adam, and Fisher nodding.

"If something had happened to you that day..." Dad shakes his head, tears in the corners of his eyes. "I don't know that she would have been able to go on. If she were here today, she would tell you that she does not regret what happened. Not at all. One thing she said to me during her health scare was, 'Better me than one of you.' She never wanted to see any of you in pain." He rests his arms on his thighs. "Sometimes I wonder if she would've been better at this than I am. If it had been me, maybe you wouldn't carry around all the scars from that day."

"No, Dad," Cade says. "It just would've been about you."

Dad nods. "It was an accident. No one is at fault, and there's nothing anyone could've done."

"I could have not gone on that ice," I murmur.

"Do any of you boys blame Chevelle?" my dad asks.

I steel myself for their answers. My stomach flips over, and I feel as though I might be sick.

"No," they say in unison, and a tear slips down my face.

"Do you worry about her all the time and the guilt that consumes her?"

"Yes," they answer.

"Chevelle, honey, you were five. I want you to think about Emelia or Trey. They're already a few years older. Would you blame them?" My dad looks me square in the eyes and waits for me to answer.

I shake my head.

"Do you believe either of your brothers would willingly die if it meant their child was safe?"

I nod, crying harder at the thought.

"Then stop blaming yourself. I know you've all forgotten certain things about your mom, but I'm here to tell you, she would be so upset to know how much guilt you carry around with you, Chevelle. Cam is a good guy, and the accident that happened last week was just that—an accident. And it turned out in our favor. We didn't lose anyone we love, and we get to be grateful to still have them in our lives."

We all remain silent.

"If life has taught you anything, it's that tragedy can strike when you least expect it, so cherish every good thing and live your life to the fullest, kids. Now, open the safe."

Fisher starts up the drill and buries it in the lock portion of the safe. It pops open. We all watch him stop the drill and pull out the bit.

I let out the breath I was holding while he was drilling.

"It's open," Cade says.

"Yeah," I say.

"Someone see what's inside," X says.

"You do it, Dad," Fisher pushes it our dad's way.

He puts the safe on the bench and opens the lid. My brothers rush over to see, but I stay back, afraid and anxious to know what's inside.

"I knew it," Adam says. "Letters." He lifts his out of the safe.

"Dad got a mixed tape." Fisher smiles.

"She loved me more," Dad says, laughing.

I edge closer. There's a note on the cassette that says, "Listen to me when you miss me." How will that go over with Marla? I shake my head because that's my dad's business, not mine.

Dad passes Cade my letter, who passes it to Adam, who passes it to me. Scripted in my mom's handwriting is *Chevelle, my darling little girl.*

"So, everyone's good, right?" Adam asks, digging his car key out of his pocket.

"Adam," I sigh.

"We're not all gonna sit here and read letters she wrote us, are we?" he says.

"No. I'm reading mine in private," Cade chimes in.

We all know Fisher won't read his here because he likes to act as though he doesn't have emotions.

"I think we'll all read on our own. And if you don't want to read it, that's okay too." Dad stands.

He's obviously crazy. I'm tearing into this as soon as I'm alone.

"Xavier, I'll hold on to yours until you're back in town," my dad says.

"Thanks, Dad. All right, everyone, I gotta get down to the field for practice. I'll chat with you later."

We all say goodbye, and he hangs up.

I say goodbye to my brothers, but my dad lingers beside me for a moment. "I'm going, but I hope you heard what I was saying earlier. At some point, you have to stop blaming yourself. What happened the other night could happen to anyone, and it has, but you got out on the good side. Be thankful and move on with your life. Cherish the things that matter. Don't push them away."

I hug my dad and squeeze him tight. "Thank you. I do feel much better."

"Good. Now I'll leave you alone." He holds up the cassette. "I have to find something to play this in. Maybe Marla will help." He heads down to his truck.

I sit on the bench in front of my mom's gravestone and open the envelope. My hands shake because I'm so nervous about what I might find inside.

"Can you believe they actually orchestrated this themselves?" I giggle because I didn't think my brothers had it in them.

I pull out the piece of paper. I never even knew her handwriting, and her cursive is so pretty.

CHEVELLE,

My baby girl. Don't tell your dad, but I had to beg him to try just one more time for a girl. Don't get me wrong, I love your brothers, but I wanted a little girl to wear cute dresses and play in my makeup. I wanted someone in our household who would under-stand me a little better. And when we found out you were a girl, you should've seen your dad's face. He was as excited as I was. Watching him with you these past three years, how you've wrapped him around your finger, has been something special.

Your fierce personality and determination to compete with your brothers are two of the traits I admire most in you. Your independence is sometimes challenging when I want you to do something, but I hope you never lose it. It will serve you well.

I'm sorry I'm gone, because we were going to be a team against the boys. But someone had other plans for me.

I think about you being the youngest and what it'll be like for you to have lost your mom so early in life. You've been with me the least amount of time, and I'm not naive enough not to know that by the time you're older, you won't remember me. Although I know your dad will do a good job of talking about me. And I hope your brothers share stories to keep my memory alive.

But just in case, I've listed some words of wisdom for you on the following pages. But if you only live life according to one specific line of advice I give you, it is, "Live your life like there isn't a tomorrow." Meaning, don't waste your time or energy worrying about things you can't control, and unfortunately, death is one of those things. If it wasn't, I'd still be with you now. Now, I'm going to put in a motherly disclaimer here—this does not mean you go out and do extreme death-defying acts. It means don't be scared to go after your dreams, to love with your entire heart, and never apologize for being you.

During the years without me, you can reference some of the things I put on the following pages, or you can just live by the one quote. Enjoy this life, Chevelle, you only get one.

Love,

Mom

I LOOK THROUGH THE PAGES, reading lines about prom and not to be a cliché by losing my virginity that night, or how all friends come with good and bad sides to them but to make sure the good outweighs the bad, and to pick a husband who loves your family as much as you do (along with a long list of the traits of a man who would deserve me).

I press the papers to my chest and take a deep breath. It feels as if she's here with me now. I can almost hear the words in her voice.

I fold the papers and put them in the envelope to read again later.

"You're probably not going to believe this, but I'm in love with Cameron Baker, Fisher's best friend…" I tell my mom all about how I fell in love with him and how scared I was when I thought I might lose him.

Something shifts inside me when I'm talking to her. A weight lifts off my shoulders and a feeling of peace wraps around me, and for the first time in as long as I can remember, I feel as if everything will work out okay.

Twenty minutes later, I stand and wipe the last of my tears. When I turn toward the street, Cam is there, waiting in front of his jeep. He waves to me. Just as my mom told me to, I decide then and there to live my life like there's no tomorrow.

I run toward his waiting arms, and he catches me as he always does. As I know he always will.

"I love you," I say once I'm secure in his arms. "I love you so much."

"I love you too, girlfriend." He lowers me to the ground, and I look up into his eyes.

"I think I like the sound of wife better."

His smile radiates joy as he brushes my hair out of my face. "Done."

Epilogue

Chevelle

A few months later...

"**Y**ou look like a winter wonderland," Nikki says, admiring me with her hand on her very swollen belly.

I look at my reflection in the mirror in the apartment above the garage at Fisher's. Everyone came together to make this a bridal suite for me, since this is the only place I could ever marry Cam. It just fits.

Cars fill the driveway, and luckily, neighbors were willing to give up their driveways for our guests to park. It took more planning, and it's not exactly ideal, but we kept our ceremony small. Or as small as you can with a family as big as mine.

I've read the advice my mom left me for my wedding, and one thing she said was to pick a meaningful place to get married. This is my day, and screw everyone else. She also said to not pick any trendy songs for my dances, pick classics, especially the father-daughter dance. I've tried to take each of her suggestions into consideration.

One thing I made my brothers incorporate into our lives

is that once a month, we get together and share stories about Mom. Even the boys have been remembering more now, and I feel as though I'm really starting to understand who my mom was.

My dad opens the door to the apartment. "Your groom just arrived."

I look out the window to catch a glimpse of him, but Cam's already gone around the side of the house.

"I'm ready." I take one last look in the mirror.

"She's more than ready. Barely needed us." Posey shakes her head.

I have no bridesmaids and he has no groomsmen, which pissed off Fisher until we had to remind him that he ran away to get married.

The Alaskan winter air hits me as soon as I walk out and follow my dad down the outside stairs. Once I'm at the bottom, I hook my arm in his, and he escorts me away to the tree-lined path that leads through the forest.

"Only you and Cam would pick an outdoor wedding in January." His breath comes out in a big white puff.

"Thanks for being a good sport."

"Anything for you, little girl," he says and kisses the top of my head.

The snow crunches under our feet as we pass the pictures we placed along the path of those Greene couples who found love before us, starting with Grandma Ethel and Grandpa, and ending with Mandi and Noah. Dad and I arrive at the clearing where lights have been hung in the trees and red hearts swing in the cold breeze. All of our guests are lined along the edge of the lake, but my eyes only search out one person.

Cam's standing on the other side of the small lake. I have

to step up on the wooden plank path my brothers and Cam built for our wedding.

"You got this," my dad whispers, tightening his hand around mine.

I think this might be as hard for him as it is for me. We follow the path lit with lanterns to the other side, where only Cam and the officiant wait.

Cam looks stunning in his dark suit and perfectly styled hair. Who knew a childhood crush could turn into real love?

My dad hands me over to Cam, then kisses my cheek and shakes Cam's hand. He quickly crosses the path back to our guests, joining Marla and my siblings.

"Ready, fiancée?"

"Really?"

"It's my last time using it," he says, and I can't help but laugh. He leans in. "I'm so proud of you," he whispers in my ear.

"Thank you."

Cam holds my hands, never letting go except for the exchange of rings. After I say my vows, he slides the wedding band on my finger, and rather than being the one we picked out together, I recognize it as my mom's.

"Oh!" My free hand flies up to cover my mouth.

"Your dad offered it to me, and I accepted. I thought it would be more meaningful for you."

I nod with tears in my eyes and glance at my dad, mouthing *thank you*. He nods with tears in his eyes, knowing what this means to me.

Each one of us kids got to pick something special from my mom's jewelry collection. I chose the first necklace my dad ever gave to my mom. And while Fisher used my mom's engagement ring to propose to Allie, my mom's wedding band has always been in my dad's possession. I assumed it would stay there. Until now.

I look at Cam and get lost in the moment with him. So much so that it feels like seconds before we're announced as husband and wife.

Cam wastes no time in dipping me and kissing me. "Love you. Wife."

Once we're announced and walk to the other side for everyone to congratulate us, my brothers work on dismantling the wooden walkway.

"Ready for what's next?" Cam asks.

After a deep breath to summon my courage, I take off my wedding skirt, leaving me in white leather pants.

"Are you serious?" His hands glide down my legs as he gets down on his knees and fits me with ice skates, lacing them up.

"You like?"

"Very much."

After he gets my skates on, he sits on one of the many benches we put up and laces his own skates.

"You know, your mom had a dream about her grandkids skating here." My dad puts his arm around Marla.

Just then, Emelia and Trey skate out, along with Jed and Adam.

Cam holds out his hand for me, and I accept it. He steps on the ice first, and I inhale another deep breath of cold Alaskan air and join him.

It takes me a while to gain my balance since it's been so many years, but as always, Cam is there to keep me steady until I find my footing. And once I do, I skate with my husband on the small family lake I haven't dared set foot on since my mom died.

Before long, the lake was crowded with our families. The

little ones slide around on their snow pants, and the speakers in the trees play the cassette my mom gave my dad in the safe.

Cam takes me in his arms. "When do we get to leave?"

"After we eat."

We chose food trucks instead of a sit-down meal. Like my mom said, it's our day to enjoy however we want.

He kisses me again. "Want to take a break?"

"Sure."

We leave the lake and take off our skates. Then he leads me back down the path through the trees.

"Are you gonna sneak me into the bridal room above the garage?"

He chuckles. "Maybe later, but first." He guides us through the cars and to the swings.

"Oh, memory lane," I say.

"The girl in the purple dress." He walks behind the swing and holds it for me.

"Damn, Fisher replaced our swing set with a fancy new one." I sit down and he sits in the swing next to me.

"At least this one will hold us. That other one was full of rust, even back then."

"You've always watched out for me."

He leans toward me, pulling the chain of my swing so I'm closer to him. "And I'll keep doing it for the rest of my life, wife."

"You better not get sick of that term since you'll be using it for the long haul."

"Oh." He smiles. "I don't know about that. There's still mom."

The End

ALSO BY PIPER RAYNE

The Baileys

Lessons from a One-Night Stand (FREE)

Advice from a Jilted Bride

Birth of a Baby Daddy

Operation Bailey Wedding (Novella)

Falling for My Brother's Best Friend

Demise of a Self-Centered Playboy

Confessions of a Naughty Nanny

Operation Bailey Babies (Novella)

Secrets of the World's Worst Matchmaker

Winning my Best Friend's Girl

Rules for Dating Your Ex

Operation Bailey Birthday (Novella)

The Greene Family

My Twist of Fortune (Free Prequel)

My Beautiful Neighbor (FREE)

My Almost Ex

My Vegas Groom

A Greene Family Summer Bash (Novella)

My Sister's Flirty Friend

My Unexpected Surprise

My Famous Frenemy

A Greene Family Vacation (Novella)

My Scorned Best Friend

My Fake Fiancé

My Brother's Forbidden Friend

A Greene Family Christmas (Novella)

Lake Starlight

The Problem with Second Chances

The Issue with Bad Boy Roommates

The Trouble with Runaway Brides

The Drawback of Single Dads

Plain Daisy Ranch

One Last Summer

The One I Left Behind

The One I Stood Beside

The One I Didn't See Coming

Modern Love

Charmed by the Bartender

Hooked by the Boxer

Mad about the Banker

Single Dads Club

Real Deal

Dirty Talker

Sexy Beast

Hollywood Hearts

Mister Mom

Animal Attraction

Domestic Bliss

Bedroom Games

Cold as Ice

On Thin Ice

Break the Ice

Chicago Law

Smitten with the Best Man

Tempted by my Ex-Husband

Seduced by my Ex's Divorce Attorney

Blue Collar Brothers

Flirting with Fire

Crushing on the Cop

Engaged to the EMT

White Collar Brothers

Sexy Filthy Boss

Dirty Flirty Enemy

Wild Steamy Hook-up

The Rooftop Crew

My Bestie's Ex

A Royal Mistake

The Rival Roomies

Our Star-Crossed Kiss

The Do-Over

A Co-Workers Crush

Hockey Hotties

Countdown to a Kiss (Free Prequel)

My Lucky #13 (FREE)

The Trouble with #9

Faking it with #41

Tropical Hat Trick (Novella)

Sneaking around with #34

Second Shot with #76

Offside with #55

Kingsmen Football Stars

False Start (Free Prequel)

You Had Your Chance, Lee Burrows

You Can't Kiss the Nanny, Brady Banks

Over My Brother's Dead Body, Chase Andrews

Chicago Grizzlies

On the Defense (Free Prequel)

Something like Hate

Something like Lust

Something like Love

The Nest

Mr. Heartbreaker

Mr. Broody

Mr. S (Title to be revealed)

Mr. C (Title to be revealed)

Holiday Romances

Single and Ready to Jingle

Claus and Effect

Merry Kissmas

Cockamamie Unicorn Ramblings

We think we can all agree that we chose the right couple to end this series. Cam and Chevelle were originally planned as book number seven in the series, but we flipped them with Xavier and Clara because we knew Cam and Chevelle had so much to work through and needed the extra time in their world to do that.

We're not sure either of us were expecting the emotion that poured into this book when we were writing. We knew Chevelle had a lot of guilt and blamed herself for her mother's death and that writing her was going to be challenging and heart wrenching. We were expecting all that.

But Cam surprised Rayne as she was writing the first draft. We all know he's a rich spoiled kid who walked into a room and owned it with his confidence. It wasn't until he came on page that Rayne discovered he didn't want to run the marina. She loved the vulnerability that came out of him with the Five Seas venture and his reluctance to allow people to see another side of him.

And then you have the two of them together. The way Cam watched out for her. The way Chevelle challenged him. The way both started to lean on the other. We were so caught up in their story, it was hard to fit in all the other Greene family members, but we think in the end it evened out. These two deserved a lot of time on the page together and it was necessary to explore what would become of the two of them as a couple.

We're sure something changed from plotting to page or something we had in mind earlier in the series, but we can't remember. With every series we have our favorites, and we can't deny that Chevelle and Cam are ours for this series.

As always, we have a lot of people to thank for getting this book into your hands...

Nina and the entire Valentine PR team.
Cassie from Joy Editing for line edits.
Ellie from My Brother's Editor for line edits.
Rosa from My Brother's Editor for proofreading.
Hang Le for the cover and branding for the entire series.
Wander Aguiar for his awesome job of photographing our muses Chevelle and Cam.
Bloggers who consistently carve out time to read, review and/or promote us.
Piper Rayne Unicorns who give us a safe space online to chat and show us love on the daily!
Readers who took the time to read our story and champion this series to other readers. We are grateful beyond words for your support and excited for what's next with our Alaska families!

Although this is the final full length Greene family book, we still have a Greene Family Christmas coming and guess what—we're moving forward twelve years in time, so you'll get to see where everyone is in the future.

And we know you're asking yourself, what about Rylan and Calista? We promise they'll be part of the novella—this is holiday you don't want to miss! They'll get their full story in, The Problem with Second Chances (Lake Starlight #1) so be sure to look for that.

A huge heartfelt thank you from both of us for embracing this series and this fictional family like your own, and for telling other readers to check it out. It truly is the biggest compliment we can receive, and we don't ever take it for granted.

xo,
Piper & Rayne

ABOUT PIPER & RAYNE

Piper Rayne is a USA Today Bestselling Author duo who write "heartwarming humor with a side of sizzle" about families, whether that be blood or found. They both have e-readers full of one-clickable books, they're married to husbands who drive them to drink, and they're both chauffeurs to their kids. Most of all, they love hot heroes and quirky heroines who make them laugh, and they hope you do, too!